GEORGE BERNARD SHAW

ARMS AND THE MAN

.

GEORGE BERNARD SHAW

ARMS AND THE MAN

ARMS AND THE MAN

BY

GEORGE BERNARD SHAW

ARMS AND THE MAN

By

GEORGE BERNARD SHAW

INTRODUCTION

To the irreverent—and which of us will claim entire exemption from that comfortable classification?—there is something very amusing in the attitude of the orthodox criticism toward Bernard Shaw. He so obviously disregards all the canons and unities and other things which every well-bred dramatist is bound to respect that his work is really unworthy of serious criticism (orthodox). Indeed he knows no more about the dramatic art than, according to his own story in "The Man of Destiny," Napoleon at Tavazzano knew of the Art of War. But both men were successes each in his way—the latter won victories and the former gained audiences, in the very teeth of the accepted theories of war and the theatre. Shaw does not know that it is unpardonable sin to have his characters make long speeches at one another, apparently thinking that this embargo applies only to long speeches which consist mainly of bombast and rhetoric. There never was an author who showed less predilection for a specific medium by which to accomplish his results. He recognized, early in his days, many things awry in the world and he assumed the task of mundane reformation with a confident spirit. It seems such a small job at twenty to set the times aright. He began as an Essayist, but who reads essays now-a-days?—he then turned novelist with no better success, for no one would read such preposterous stuff as he chose to emit. He only succeeded in proving that absolutely rational men and women—although he has created few of the latter—can be most extremely disagreeable to our conventional way of thinking.

As a last resort, he turned to the stage, not that he cared for the dramatic art, for no man seems to care less about "Art for Art's sake," being in this a perfect foil to his brilliant compatriot and contemporary, Wilde. He cast his theories in dramatic forms merely because no other course except silence or physical revolt was open to him. For a long time it seemed as if this resource too was doomed to fail him. But finally he has attained a hearing and now attempts at suppression merely serve to advertise their victim.

It will repay those who seek analogies in literature to compare Shaw with Cervantes. After a life of heroic endeavor, disappointment, slavery, and poverty, the author of "Don Quixote" gave the world a serious work which caused to be laughed off the world's stage forever the final vestiges of decadent chivalry.

The institution had long been outgrown, but its vernacular continued to be the speech and to express the thought "of the world and among the vulgar," as the quaint, old novelist puts it, just as to-day the novel intended for the consumption of the unenlightened must deal with peers and millionaires and be dressed in stilted language. Marvellously he succeeded, but in a way he least intended. We have not yet, after so many years, determined whether it is a work to laugh or cry over. "It is our joyfullest modern book," says Carlyle, while Landor thinks that "readers who see nothing more than a burlesque in 'Don Quixote' have but shallow appreciation of the work."

Shaw in like manner comes upon the scene when many of our social usages are outworn. He sees the fact, announces it, and we burst into guffaws. The continuous laughter which greets Shaw's plays arises from a real contrast in the point of view of the dramatist and his audiences. When Pinero or Jones describes a whimsical situation we never doubt for a moment that the author's point of view is our own and that the abnormal predicament of his characters appeals to him in the same light as to his audience. With Shaw this sense of community of feeling is wholly lacking. He describes things as he sees them, and the house is in a roar. Who is right? If we were really using our own senses and not gazing through the glasses of convention and romance and make-believe, should we see things as Shaw does?

Must it not cause Shaw to doubt his own or the public's sanity to hear audiences laughing boisterously over tragic situations? And yet, if they did not come to laugh, they would not come at all. Mockery is the price he must pay for a hearing. Or has he calculated to a nicety the power of reaction? Does he seek to drive us to aspiration by the portrayal of sordidness, to disinterestedness by the picture of selfishness, to illusion by disillusionment? It is impossible to believe that he is unconscious of the humor of his dramatic situations, yet he stoically gives no sign. He even dares the charge, terrible in proportion to its truth, which the most serious of us shrinks from—the lack of a sense of humor. Men would rather have their integrity impugned.

In "Arms and the Man" the subject which occupies the dramatist's attention is that survival of barbarity—militarism—which raises its horrid head from time to time to cast a doubt on the reality of our civilization. No more hoary superstition survives than that the donning of a uniform changes the nature of the wearer. This notion pervades society to such an extent that when we find some soldiers placed upon the stage acting rationally, our conventionalized senses are shocked. The only men who have no illusions about war are those who have recently been there, and, of course, Mr. Shaw, who has no illusions about anything.

It is hard to speak too highly of "Candida." No equally subtle and incisive study of domestic relations exists in the English drama. One has to turn to George Meredith's "The Egoist" to find such character dissection. The central note of the play is, that with the true woman, weakness which appeals to the maternal instinct is more powerful than strength which offers protection. Candida is quite unpoetic, as, indeed, with rare exceptions, women are prone to be. They have small delight in poetry, but are the stuff of which poems and dreams are made. The husband glorying in his strength but convicted of his weakness, the poet pitiful in his physical impotence but strong in his perception of truth, the hopelessly demoralized manufacturer, the conventional and hence emotional typist make up a group which the drama of any language may be challenged to rival.

In "The Man of Destiny" the object of the dramatist is not so much the destruction as the explanation of the Napoleonic tradition, which has so powerfully influenced generation after generation for a century. However the man may be regarded, he was a miracle. Shaw shows that he achieved his extraordinary career by suspending, for himself, the pressure of the moral and conventional atmosphere, while leaving it operative for others. Those who study this play—extravaganza, that it is—will attain a clearer comprehension of Napoleon than they can get from all the biographies.

"You Never Can Tell" offers an amusing study of the play of social conventions. The "twins" illustrate the disconcerting effects of that perfect frankness which would make life intolerable. Gloria demonstrates the powerlessness of reason to overcome natural instincts. The idea that parental duties and functions can be fulfilled by the light of such knowledge as man and woman attain by intuition is brilliantly lampooned. Crampton, the father, typifies the common superstition that among the privileges of parenthood are inflexibility, tyranny, and respect, the last entirely regardless of whether it has been deserved.

The waiter, William, is the best illustration of the man "who knows his place" that the stage has seen. He is the most pathetic figure of the play. One touch of verisimilitude is lacking; none of the guests gives him a tip, yet he maintains his urbanity. As Mr. Shaw has not yet visited America he may be unaware of the improbability of this situation.

To those who regard literary men merely as purveyors of amusement for people who have not wit enough to entertain themselves, Ibsen and Shaw, Maeterlinck and Gorky must remain enigmas. It is so much pleasanter to ignore than to face unpleasant realities—to take Riverside Drive and not Mulberry Street as the exponent of our life and the expression of our civilization. These men are the sappers and miners of the advancing army of justice. The audience which demands the truth and despises the contemptible conventions that dominate alike our stage and our life is daily growing. Shaw and men like him—if indeed he is not absolutely unique—will not for the future lack a hearing.

M.

ACT I

Night. A lady's bedchamber in Bulgaria, in a small town near the Dragoman Pass. It is late in November in the year 1885, and through an open window with a little balcony on the left can be seen a peak of the Balkans, wonderfully white and beautiful in the starlit snow. The interior of the room is not like anything to be seen in the east of Europe. It is half rich Bulgarian, half cheap Viennese. The counterpane and hangings of the bed, the window curtains, the little carpet, and all the ornamental textile fabrics in the room are oriental and gorgeous: the paper on the walls is occidental and paltry. Above the head of the bed, which stands against a little wall cutting off the right hand corner of the room diagonally, is a painted wooden shrine, blue and gold, with an ivory image of Christ, and a light hanging before it in a pierced metal ball suspended by three chains. On the left, further forward, is an ottoman. The washstand, against the wall on the left, consists of an enamelled iron basin with a pail beneath it in a painted metal frame, and a single towel on the rail at the side. A chair near it is Austrian bent wood, with cane seat. The dressing table, between the bed and the window, is an ordinary pine table, covered with a cloth of many colors, but with an expensive toilet mirror on it. The door is on the right; and there is a chest of drawers between the door and the bed. This chest of drawers is also covered by a variegated native cloth, and on it there is a pile of paper backed novels, a box of chocolate creams, and a miniature easel, on which is a large photograph of an extremely handsome officer, whose lofty bearing and magnetic glance can be felt even from the portrait. The room is lighted by a candle on the chest of drawers, and another on the dressing table, with a box of matches beside it.

The window is hinged doorwise and stands wide open, folding back to the left. Outside a pair of wooden shutters, opening outwards, also stand open. On the balcony, a young lady, intensely conscious of the romantic beauty of the night, and of the fact that her own youth and beauty is a part of it, is on the balcony, gazing at the snowy Balkans. She is covered by a long mantle of furs, worth, on a moderate estimate, about three times the furniture of her room.

Her reverie is interrupted by her mother, Catherine Petkoff, a woman over forty, imperiously energetic, with magnificent black hair and eyes, who might be a very splendid specimen of the wife of a mountain farmer, but is determined to be a Viennese lady, and to that end wears a fashionable tea gown on all occasions.

CATHERINE (entering hastily, full of good news). Raina—(she pronounces it Rah-eena, with the stress on the ee) Raina—(she goes to the bed, expecting to find Raina there.) Why, where—(Raina looks into the room.) Heavens! child, are you out in the night air instead of in your bed? You'll catch your death. Louka told me you were asleep.

RAINA (coming in). I sent her away. I wanted to be alone. The stars are so beautiful! What is the matter?

CATHERINE. Such news. There has been a battle!

RAINA (her eyes dilating). Ah! (She throws the cloak on the ottoman, and comes eagerly to Catherine in her nightgown, a pretty garment, but evidently the only one she has on.)

CATHERINE. A great battle at Slivnitza! A victory! And it was won by Sergius.

RAINA (with a cry of delight). Ah! (Rapturously.) Oh, mother! (Then, with sudden anxiety) Is father safe?

CATHERINE. Of course: he sent me the news. Sergius is the hero of the hour, the idol of the regiment.

RAINA. Tell me, tell me. How was it! (Ecstatically) Oh, mother, mother, mother! (Raina pulls her mother down on the ottoman; and they kiss one another frantically.)

CATHERINE (with surging enthusiasm). You can't guess how splendid it is. A cavalry charge—think of that! He defied our Russian commanders—acted without orders—led a charge on his own responsibility—headed it himself—was the first man to sweep through their guns. Can't you see it, Raina; our gallant splendid Bulgarians with their swords and eyes flashing, thundering down like an avalanche and scattering the wretched Servian dandies like chaff. And you—you kept Sergius waiting a year before you would be betrothed to him. Oh, if you have a drop of Bulgarian blood in your veins, you will worship him when he comes back.

RAINA. What will he care for my poor little worship after the acclamations of a whole army of heroes? But no matter: I am so happy—so proud! (She rises and walks about excitedly.) It proves that all our ideas were real after all.

CATHERINE (indignantly). Our ideas real! What do you mean?

RAINA. Our ideas of what Sergius would do—our patriotism—our heroic ideals. Oh, what faithless little creatures girls are!—I sometimes used to doubt whether they were anything but dreams. When I buckled on Sergius's sword he looked so noble: it was treason to think of disillusion or humiliation or failure. And yet—and yet—(Quickly.) Promise me you'll never tell him.

CATHERINE. Don't ask me for promises until I know what I am promising.

RAINA. Well, it came into my head just as he was holding me in his arms and looking into my eyes, that perhaps we only had our heroic ideas because we are so fond of reading Byron and Pushkin, and because we were so delighted with the opera that season at Bucharest. Real life is so seldom like that—indeed never, as far as I knew it then. (Remorsefully.) Only think, mother, I doubted him: I wondered whether all his heroic qualities and his soldiership might not prove mere imagination when he went into a real battle. I had an uneasy fear that he might cut a poor figure there beside all those clever Russian officers.

2

CATHERINE. A poor figure! Shame on you! The Servians have Austrian officers who are just as clever as our Russians; but we have beaten them in every battle for all that.

RAINA (laughing and sitting down again). Yes, I was only a prosaic little coward. Oh, to think that it was all true—that Sergius is just as splendid and noble as he looks—that the world is really a glorious world for women who can see its glory and men who can act its romance! What happiness! what unspeakable fulfilment! Ah! (She throws herself on her knees beside her mother and flings her arms passionately round her. They are interrupted by the entry of Louka, a handsome, proud girl in a pretty Bulgarian peasant's dress with double apron, so defiant that her servility to Raina is almost insolent. She is afraid of Catherine, but even with her goes as far as she dares. She is just now excited like the others; but she has no sympathy for Raina's raptures and looks contemptuously at the ecstasies of the two before she addresses them.)

LOUKA. If you please, madam, all the windows are to be closed and the shutters made fast. They say there may be shooting in the streets. (Raina and Catherine rise together, alarmed.) The Servians are being chased right back through the pass; and they say they may run into the town. Our cavalry will be after them; and our people will be ready for them you may be sure, now that they are running away. (She goes out on the balcony and pulls the outside shutters to; then steps back into the room.)

RAINA. I wish our people were not so cruel. What glory is there in killing wretched fugitives?

CATHERINE (business-like, her housekeeping instincts aroused). I must see that everything is made safe downstairs.

RAINA (to Louka). Leave the shutters so that I can just close them if I hear any noise.

CATHERINE (authoritatively, turning on her way to the door). Oh, no, dear, you must keep them fastened. You would be sure to drop off to sleep and leave them open. Make them fast, Louka.

LOUKA. Yes, madam. (She fastens them.)

RAINA. Don't be anxious about me. The moment I hear a shot, I shall blow out the candles and roll myself up in bed with my ears well covered.

CATHERINE. Quite the wisest thing you can do, my love. Good-night.

RAINA. Good-night. (They kiss one another, and Raina's emotion comes back for a moment.) Wish me joy of the happiest night of my life—if only there are no fugitives.

CATHERINE. Go to bed, dear; and don't think of them. (She goes out.)

LOUKA (secretly, to Raina). If you would like the shutters open, just give them a push like this. (She pushes them: they open: she pulls them to again.) One of them ought to be bolted at the bottom; but the bolt's gone.

RAINA (with dignity, reproving her). Thanks, Louka; but we must do what we are told. (Louka makes a grimace.) Good-night.

LOUKA (carelessly). Good-night. (She goes out, swaggering.)

(Raina, left alone, goes to the chest of drawers, and adores the portrait there with feelings that are beyond all expression. She does not kiss it or press it to her breast, or shew it any mark of bodily affection; but she takes it in her hands and elevates it like a priestess.)

RAINA (looking up at the picture with worship.) Oh, I shall never be unworthy of you any more, my hero—never, never, never.

(She replaces it reverently, and selects a novel from the little pile of books. She turns over the leaves dreamily; finds her page; turns the book inside out at it; and then, with a happy sigh, gets into bed and prepares to read herself to sleep. But before abandoning herself to fiction, she raises her eyes once more, thinking of the blessed reality and murmurs)

My hero! my hero!

(A distant shot breaks the quiet of the night outside. She starts, listening; and two more shots, much nearer, follow, startling her so that she scrambles out of bed, and hastily blows out the candle on the chest of drawers. Then, putting her fingers in her ears, she runs to the dressing-table and blows out the light there, and hurries back to bed. The room is now in darkness: nothing is visible but the glimmer of the light in the pierced ball before the image, and the starlight seen through the slits at the top of the shutters. The firing breaks out again: there is a startling fusillade quite close at hand. Whilst it is still echoing, the shutters disappear, pulled open from without, and for an instant the rectangle of snowy starlight flashes out with the figure of a man in black upon it. The shutters close immediately and the room is dark again. But the silence is now broken by the sound of panting. Then there is a scrape; and the flame of a match is seen in the middle of the room.)

RAINA (crouching on the bed). Who's there? (The match is out instantly.) Who's there? Who is that?

A MAN'S VOICE (in the darkness, subduedly, but threateningly). Sh—sh! Don't call out or you'll be shot. Be good; and no harm will happen to you. (She is heard leaving her bed, and making for the door.) Take care, there's no use in trying to run away. Remember, if you raise your voice my pistol will go off. (Commandingly.) Strike a light and let me see you. Do you hear? (Another moment of silence and darkness. Then she is heard retreating to the dressing-table. She lights a candle, and the mystery is at an end. A man of about 35, in a deplorable plight, bespattered with mud and blood and snow, his belt and the strap of his revolver case keeping together the torn ruins of the blue coat of a Servian artillery officer. As far as the candlelight and his unwashed, unkempt condition make it possible to judge, he is a man of middling stature and undistinguished appearance, with strong neck and shoulders, a roundish, obstinate looking head covered with short crisp bronze curls, clear quick blue eyes and good brows and mouth, a hopelessly prosaic nose like that of a strong-minded baby, trim soldierlike carriage and energetic manner, and with all his wits about him in spite of his desperate predicament—even with a sense of humor of it, without, however, the least intention of trifling with it or throwing away a chance. He reckons up what he can guess about Raina—her age, her social position, her character, the extent to which she is frightened—at a glance, and continues, more politely but still most determinedly) Excuse my disturbing you; but you recognise my uniform—Servian. If I'm caught I shall be killed. (Determinedly.) Do you understand that?

RAINA. Yes.

MAN. Well, I don't intend to get killed if I can help it. (Still more determinedly.) Do you understand that? (He locks the door with a snap.)

RAINA (disdainfully). I suppose not. (She draws herself up superbly, and looks him straight in the face, saying with emphasis) Some soldiers, I know, are afraid of death.

MAN (with grim goodhumor). All of them, dear lady, all of them, believe me. It is our duty to live as long as we can, and kill as many of the enemy as we can. Now if you raise an alarm—

RAINA (cutting him short). You will shoot me. How do you know that I am afraid to die?

MAN (cunningly). Ah; but suppose I don't shoot you, what will happen then? Why, a lot of your cavalry—the greatest blackguards in your army—will burst into this pretty room of yours and slaughter me here like a pig; for I'll fight like a demon: they shan't get me into the street to amuse themselves with: I know what they are. Are you prepared to receive that sort of company in your present undress? (Raina, suddenly conscious of her nightgown, instinctively shrinks and gathers it more closely about her. He watches her, and adds, pitilessly) It's rather scanty, eh? (She turns to the ottoman. He raises his pistol instantly, and cries) Stop! (She stops.) Where are you going?

RAINA (with dignified patience). Only to get my cloak.

MAN (darting to the ottoman and snatching the cloak). A good idea. No: I'll keep the cloak: and you will take care that nobody comes in and sees you without it. This is a better weapon than the pistol. (He throws the pistol down on the ottoman.)

RAINA (revolted). It is not the weapon of a gentleman!

MAN. It's good enough for a man with only you to stand between him and death. (As they look at one another for a moment, Raina hardly able to believe that even a Servian officer can be so cynically and selfishly unchivalrous, they are startled by a sharp fusillade in the street. The chill of imminent death hushes the man's voice as he adds) Do you hear? If you are going to bring those scoundrels in on me you shall receive them as you are. (Raina meets his eye with unflinching scorn. Suddenly he starts, listening. There is a step outside. Someone tries the door, and then knocks hurriedly and urgently at it. Raina looks at the man, breathless. He throws up his head with the gesture of a man who sees that it is all over with him, and, dropping the manner which he has been assuming to intimidate her, flings the cloak to her, exclaiming, sincerely and kindly) No use: I'm done for. Quick! wrap yourself up: they're coming!

RAINA (catching the cloak eagerly). Oh, thank you. (She wraps herself up with great relief. He draws his sabre and turns to the door, waiting.)

LOUKA (outside, knocking). My lady, my lady! Get up, quick, and open the door.

RAINA (anxiously). What will you do?

MAN (grimly). Never mind. Keep out of the way. It will not last long.

RAINA (impulsively). I'll help you. Hide yourself, oh, hide yourself, quick, behind the curtain. (She seizes him by a torn strip of his sleeve, and pulls him towards the window.)

MAN (yielding to her). There is just half a chance, if you keep your head. Remember: nine soldiers out of ten are born fools. (He hides behind the curtain, looking out for a moment to say, finally) If they find me, I promise you a fight—a devil of a fight! (He disappears. Raina takes of the cloak and throws it across the foot of the bed. Then with a sleepy, disturbed air, she opens the door. Louka enters excitedly.)

LOUKA. A man has been seen climbing up the water-pipe to your balcony—a Servian. The soldiers want to search for him; and they are so wild and drunk and furious. My lady says you are to dress at once.

RAINA (as if annoyed at being disturbed). They shall not search here. Why have they been let in?

CATHERINE (coming in hastily). Raina, darling, are you safe? Have you seen anyone or heard anything?

RAINA. I heard the shooting. Surely the soldiers will not dare come in here?

CATHERINE. I have found a Russian officer, thank Heaven: he knows Sergius. (Speaking through the door to someone outside.) Sir, will you come in now! My daughter is ready.

(A young Russian officer, in Bulgarian uniform, enters, sword in hand.)

THE OFFICER. (with soft, feline politeness and stiff military carriage). Good evening, gracious lady; I am sorry to intrude, but there is a fugitive hiding on the balcony. Will you and the gracious lady your mother please to withdraw whilst we search?

RAINA (petulantly). Nonsense, sir, you can see that there is no one on the balcony. (She throws the shutters wide open and stands with her back to the curtain where the man is hidden, pointing to the moonlit balcony. A couple of shots are fired right under the window, and a bullet shatters the glass opposite Raina, who winks and gasps, but stands her ground, whilst Catherine screams, and the officer rushes to the balcony.)

THE OFFICER. (on the balcony, shouting savagely down to the street). Cease firing there, you fools: do you hear? Cease firing, damn you. (He glares down for a moment; then turns to Raina, trying to resume his polite manner.) Could anyone have got in without your knowledge? Were you asleep?

RAINA. No, I have not been to bed.

THE OFFICER. (impatiently, coming back into the room). Your neighbours have their heads so full of runaway Servians that they see them everywhere. (Politely.) Gracious lady, a thousand pardons. Good-night. (Military bow, which Raina returns coldly. Another to Catherine, who follows him out. Raina closes the shutters. She turns and sees Louka, who has been watching the scene curiously.)

RAINA. Don't leave my mother, Louka, whilst the soldiers are here. (Louka glances at Raina, at the ottoman, at the curtain; then purses her lips secretively, laughs to herself, and goes out. Raina follows her to the door, shuts it behind her with a slam, and locks it violently. The man immediately steps out from behind the curtain, sheathing his sabre, and dismissing the danger from his mind in a businesslike way.)

MAN. A narrow shave; but a miss is as good as a mile. Dear young lady, your servant until death. I wish for your sake I had joined the Bulgarian army instead of the Servian. I am not a native Servian.

RAINA (haughtily). No, you are one of the Austrians who set the Servians on to rob us of our national liberty, and who officer their army for them. We hate them!

MAN. Austrian! not I. Don't hate me, dear young lady. I am only a Swiss, fighting merely as a professional soldier. I joined Servia because it was nearest to me. Be generous: you've beaten us hollow.

RAINA. Have I not been generous?

MAN. Noble!—heroic! But I'm not saved yet. This particular rush will soon pass through; but the pursuit will go on all night by fits and starts. I must take my chance to get off during a quiet interval. You don't mind my waiting just a minute or two, do you?

RAINA. Oh, no: I am sorry you will have to go into danger again. (Motioning towards ottoman.) Won't you sit—(She breaks off with an irrepressible cry of alarm as she catches sight of the pistol. The man, all nerves, shies like a frightened horse.)

MAN (irritably). Don't frighten me like that. What is it?

RAINA. Your pistol! It was staring that officer in the face all the time. What an escape!

MAN (vexed at being unnecessarily terrified). Oh, is that all?

RAINA (staring at him rather superciliously, conceiving a poorer and poorer opinion of him, and feeling proportionately more and more at her ease with him). I am sorry I frightened you. (She takes up the pistol and hands it to him.) Pray take it to protect yourself against me.

MAN (grinning wearily at the sarcasm as he takes the pistol). No use, dear young lady: there's nothing in it. It's not loaded. (He makes a grimace at it, and drops it disparagingly into his revolver case.)

RAINA. Load it by all means.

MAN. I've no ammunition. What use are cartridges in battle? I always carry chocolate instead; and I finished the last cake of that yesterday.

RAINA (outraged in her most cherished ideals of manhood). Chocolate! Do you stuff your pockets with sweets—like a schoolboy—even in the field?

MAN. Yes. Isn't it contemptible?

(Raina stares at him, unable to utter her feelings. Then she sails away scornfully to the chest of drawers, and returns with the box of confectionery in her hand.)

RAINA. Allow me. I am sorry I have eaten them all except these. (She offers him the box.)

MAN (ravenously). You're an angel! (He gobbles the comfits.) Creams! Delicious! (He looks anxiously to see whether there are any more. There are none. He accepts the inevitable with pathetic goodhumor, and says, with grateful emotion) Bless you, dear lady. You can always tell an old soldier by the inside of his holsters and cartridge boxes. The young ones carry pistols and cartridges; the old ones, grub. Thank you. (He hands back the box. She snatches it contemptuously from him and throws it away. This impatient action is so sudden that he shies again.) Ugh! Don't do things so suddenly, gracious lady. Don't revenge yourself because I frightened you just now.

RAINA (superbly). Frighten me! Do you know, sir, that though I am only a woman, I think I am at heart as brave as you.

MAN. I should think so. You haven't been under fire for three days as I have. I can stand two days without shewing it much; but no man can stand three days: I'm as nervous as a mouse. (He sits down on the ottoman, and takes his head in his hands.) Would you like to see me cry?

RAINA (quickly). No.

MAN. If you would, all you have to do is to scold me just as if I were a little boy and you my nurse. If I were in camp now they'd play all sorts of tricks on me.

RAINA (a little moved). I'm sorry. I won't scold you. (Touched by the sympathy in her tone, he raises his head and looks gratefully at her: she immediately draws hack and says stiffly) You must excuse me: our soldiers are not like that. (She moves away from the ottoman.)

MAN. Oh, yes, they are. There are only two sorts of soldiers: old ones and young ones. I've served fourteen years: half of your fellows never smelt powder before. Why, how is it that you've just beaten us? Sheer ignorance of the art of war, nothing else. (Indignantly.) I never saw anything so unprofessional.

RAINA (ironically). Oh, was it unprofessional to beat you?

MAN. Well, come, is it professional to throw a regiment of cavalry on a battery of machine guns, with the dead certainty that if the guns go off not a horse or man will ever get within fifty yards of the fire? I couldn't believe my eyes when I saw it.

RAINA (eagerly turning to him, as all her enthusiasm and her dream of glory rush back on her). Did you see the great cavalry charge? Oh, tell me about it. Describe it to me.

MAN. You never saw a cavalry charge, did you?

RAINA. How could I?

MAN. Ah, perhaps not—of course. Well, it's a funny sight. It's like slinging a handful of peas against a window pane: first one comes; then two or three close behind him; and then all the rest in a lump.

RAINA (her eyes dilating as she raises her clasped hands ecstatically). Yes, first One!—the bravest of the brave!

MAN (prosaically). Hm! you should see the poor devil pulling at his horse.

RAINA. Why should he pull at his horse?

MAN (impatient of so stupid a question). It's running away with him, of course: do you suppose the fellow wants to get there before the others and be killed? Then they all come. You can tell the young ones by their wildness and their slashing. The old ones come

9

bunched up under the number one guard: they know that they are mere projectiles, and that it's no use trying to fight. The wounds are mostly broken knees, from the horses cannoning together.

RAINA. Ugh! But I don't believe the first man is a coward. I believe he is a hero!

MAN (goodhumoredly). That's what you'd have said if you'd seen the first man in the charge to-day.

RAINA (breathless). Ah, I knew it! Tell me—tell me about him.

MAN. He did it like an operatic tenor—a regular handsome fellow, with flashing eyes and lovely moustache, shouting a war-cry and charging like Don Quixote at the windmills. We nearly burst with laughter at him; but when the sergeant ran up as white as a sheet, and told us they'd sent us the wrong cartridges, and that we couldn't fire a shot for the next ten minutes, we laughed at the other side of our mouths. I never felt so sick in my life, though I've been in one or two very tight places. And I hadn't even a revolver cartridge—nothing but chocolate. We'd no bayonets—nothing. Of course, they just cut us to bits. And there was Don Quixote flourishing like a drum major, thinking he'd done the cleverest thing ever known, whereas he ought to be courtmartialled for it. Of all the fools ever let loose on a field of battle, that man must be the very maddest. He and his regiment simply committed suicide—only the pistol missed fire, that's all.

RAINA (deeply wounded, but steadfastly loyal to her ideals). Indeed! Would you know him again if you saw him?

MAN. Shall I ever forget him. (She again goes to the chest of drawers. He watches her with a vague hope that she may have something else for him to eat. She takes the portrait from its stand and brings it to him.)

RAINA. That is a photograph of the gentleman—the patriot and hero—to whom I am betrothed.

MAN (looking at it). I'm really very sorry. (Looking at her.) Was it fair to lead me on? (He looks at the portrait again.) Yes: that's him: not a doubt of it. (He stifles a laugh.)

RAINA (quickly). Why do you laugh?

MAN (shamefacedly, but still greatly tickled). I didn't laugh, I assure you. At least I didn't mean to. But when I think of him charging the windmills and thinking he was doing the finest thing—(chokes with suppressed laughter).

RAINA (sternly). Give me back the portrait, sir.

MAN (with sincere remorse). Of course. Certainly. I'm really very sorry. (She deliberately kisses it, and looks him straight in the face, before returning to the chest of drawers to replace it. He follows her, apologizing.) Perhaps I'm quite wrong, you know: no doubt I am. Most likely he had got wind of the cartridge business somehow, and knew it was a safe job.

RAINA. That is to say, he was a pretender and a coward! You did not dare say that before.

MAN (with a comic gesture of despair). It's no use, dear lady: I can't make you see it from the professional point of view. (As he turns away to get back to the ottoman, the firing begins again in the distance.)

RAINA (sternly, as she sees him listening to the shots). So much the better for you.

MAN (turning). How?

RAINA. You are my enemy; and you are at my mercy. What would I do if I were a professional soldier?

MAN. Ah, true, dear young lady: you're always right. I know how good you have been to me: to my last hour I shall remember those three chocolate creams. It was unsoldierly; but it was angelic.

RAINA (coldly). Thank you. And now I will do a soldierly thing. You cannot stay here after what you have just said about my future husband; but I will go out on the balcony and see whether it is safe for you to climb down into the street. (She turns to the window.)

MAN (changing countenance). Down that waterpipe! Stop! Wait! I can't! I daren't! The very thought of it makes me giddy. I came up it fast enough with death behind me. But to face it now in cold blood!—(He sinks on the ottoman.) It's no use: I give up: I'm beaten. Give the alarm. (He drops his head in his hands in the deepest dejection.)

RAINA (disarmed by pity). Come, don't be disheartened. (She stoops over him almost maternally: he shakes his head.) Oh, you are a very poor soldier—a chocolate cream soldier. Come, cheer up: it takes less courage to climb down than to face capture—remember that.

MAN (dreamily, lulled by her voice). No, capture only means death; and death is sleep—oh, sleep, sleep, sleep, undisturbed sleep! Climbing down the pipe means doing something— exerting myself—thinking! Death ten times over first.

RAINA (softly and wonderingly, catching the rhythm of his weariness). Are you so sleepy as that?

MAN. I've not had two hours' undisturbed sleep since the war began. I'm on the staff: you don't know what that means. I haven't closed my eyes for thirty-six hours.

RAINA (desperately). But what am I to do with you.

MAN (staggering up). Of course I must do something. (He shakes himself; pulls himself together; and speaks with rallied vigour and courage.) You see, sleep or no sleep, hunger or no hunger, tired or not tired, you can always do a thing when you know it must be done. Well, that pipe must be got down—(He hits himself on the chest, and adds)—Do you hear that, you chocolate cream soldier? (He turns to the window.)

RAINA (anxiously). But if you fall?

MAN. I shall sleep as if the stones were a feather bed. Good-bye. (He makes boldly for the window, and his hand is on the shutter when there is a terrible burst of firing in the street beneath.)

RAINA (rushing to him). Stop! (She catches him by the shoulder, and turns him quite round.) They'll kill you.

MAN (coolly, but attentively). Never mind: this sort of thing is all in my day's work. I'm bound to take my chance. (Decisively.) Now do what I tell you. Put out the candles, so that they shan't see the light when I open the shutters. And keep away from the window, whatever you do. If they see me, they're sure to have a shot at me.

RAINA (clinging to him). They're sure to see you: it's bright moonlight. I'll save you—oh, how can you be so indifferent? You want me to save you, don't you?

MAN. I really don't want to be troublesome. (She shakes him in her impatience.) I am not indifferent, dear young lady, I assure you. But how is it to be done?

RAINA. Come away from the window—please. (She coaxes him back to the middle of the room. He submits humbly. She releases him, and addresses him patronizingly.) Now listen. You must trust to our hospitality. You do not yet know in whose house you are. I am a Petkoff.

MAN. What's that?

RAINA (rather indignantly). I mean that I belong to the family of the Petkoffs, the richest and best known in our country.

MAN. Oh, yes, of course. I beg your pardon. The Petkoffs, to be sure. How stupid of me!

RAINA. You know you never heard of them until this minute. How can you stoop to pretend?

MAN. Forgive me: I'm too tired to think; and the change of subject was too much for me. Don't scold me.

RAINA. I forgot. It might make you cry. (He nods, quite seriously. She pouts and then resumes her patronizing tone.) I must tell you that my father holds the highest command of any Bulgarian in our army. He is (proudly) a Major.

MAN (pretending to be deeply impressed). A Major! Bless me! Think of that!

RAINA. You shewed great ignorance in thinking that it was necessary to climb up to the balcony, because ours is the only private house that has two rows of windows. There is a flight of stairs inside to get up and down by.

MAN. Stairs! How grand! You live in great luxury indeed, dear young lady.

RAINA. Do you know what a library is?

MAN. A library? A roomful of books.

RAINA. Yes, we have one, the only one in Bulgaria.

MAN. Actually a real library! I should like to see that.

RAINA (affectedly). I tell you these things to shew you that you are not in the house of ignorant country folk who would kill you the moment they saw your Servian uniform, but among civilized people. We go to Bucharest every year for the opera season; and I have spent a whole month in Vienna.

MAN. I saw that, dear young lady. I saw at once that you knew the world.

RAINA. Have you ever seen the opera of Ernani?

MAN. Is that the one with the devil in it in red velvet, and a soldier's chorus?

RAINA (contemptuously). No!

MAN (stifling a heavy sigh of weariness). Then I don't know it.

RAINA. I thought you might have remembered the great scene where Ernani, flying from his foes just as you are tonight, takes refuge in the castle of his bitterest enemy, an old Castilian noble. The noble refuses to give him up. His guest is sacred to him.

MAN (quickly waking up a little). Have your people got that notion?

RAINA (with dignity). My mother and I can understand that notion, as you call it. And if instead of threatening me with your pistol as you did, you had simply thrown yourself as a fugitive on our hospitality, you would have been as safe as in your father's house.

MAN. Quite sure?

RAINA (turning her back on him in disgust.) Oh, it is useless to try and make you understand.

MAN. Don't be angry: you see how awkward it would be for me if there was any mistake. My father is a very hospitable man: he keeps six hotels; but I couldn't trust him as far as that. What about YOUR father?

RAINA. He is away at Slivnitza fighting for his country. I answer for your safety. There is my hand in pledge of it. Will that reassure you? (She offers him her hand.)

MAN (looking dubiously at his own hand). Better not touch my hand, dear young lady. I must have a wash first.

RAINA (touched). That is very nice of you. I see that you are a gentleman.

MAN (puzzled). Eh?

RAINA. You must not think I am surprised. Bulgarians of really good standing—people in OUR position—wash their hands nearly every day. But I appreciate your delicacy. You may take my hand. (She offers it again.)

MAN (kissing it with his hands behind his back). Thanks, gracious young lady: I feel safe at last. And now would you mind breaking the news to your mother? I had better not stay here secretly longer than is necessary.

RAINA. If you will be so good as to keep perfectly still whilst I am away.

MAN. Certainly. (He sits down on the ottoman.)

(Raina goes to the bed and wraps herself in the fur cloak. His eyes close. She goes to the door, but on turning for a last look at him, sees that he is dropping of to sleep.)

RAINA (at the door). You are not going asleep, are you? (He murmurs inarticulately: she runs to him and shakes him.) Do you hear? Wake up: you are falling asleep.

MAN. Eh? Falling aslee—? Oh, no, not the least in the world: I was only thinking. It's all right: I'm wide awake.

RAINA (severely). Will you please stand up while I am away. (He rises reluctantly.) All the time, mind.

MAN (standing unsteadily). Certainly—certainly: you may depend on me.

(Raina looks doubtfully at him. He smiles foolishly. She goes reluctant, turning again at the door, and almost catching him in the act of yawning. She goes out.)

MAN (drowsily). Sleep, sleep, sleep, sleep, slee—(The words trail off into a murmur. He wakes again with a shock on the point of falling.) Where am I? That's what I want to know: where am I? Must keep awake. Nothing keeps me awake except danger—remember that—

(intently) danger, danger, danger, dan— Where's danger? Must find it. (He starts of vaguely around the room in search of it.) What am I looking for? Sleep—danger—don't know. (He stumbles against the bed.) Ah, yes: now I know. All right now. I'm to go to bed, but not to sleep—be sure not to sleep—because of danger. Not to lie down, either, only sit down. (He sits on the bed. A blissful expression comes into his face.) Ah! (With a happy sigh he sinks back at full length; lifts his boots into the bed with a final effort; and falls fast asleep instantly.)

(Catherine comes in, followed by Raina.)

RAINA (looking at the ottoman). He's gone! I left him here.

CATHERINE, Here! Then he must have climbed down from the—

RAINA (seeing him). Oh! (She points.)

CATHERINE (scandalized). Well! (She strides to the left side of the bed, Raina following and standing opposite her on the right.) He's fast asleep. The brute!

RAINA (anxiously). Sh!

CATHERINE (shaking him). Sir! (Shaking him again, harder.) Sir!! (Vehemently shaking very bard.) Sir!!!

RAINA (catching her arm). Don't, mamma: the poor dear is worn out. Let him sleep.

CATHERINE (letting him go and turning amazed to Raina). The poor dear! Raina!!! (She looks sternly at her daughter. The man sleeps profoundly.)

ACT II

The sixth of March, 1886. In the garden of major Petkoff's house. It is a fine spring morning; and the garden looks fresh and pretty. Beyond the paling the tops of a couple of minarets can be seen, shewing that there is a valley there, with the little town in it. A few miles further the Balkan mountains rise and shut in the view. Within the garden the side of the house is seen on the right, with a garden door reached by a little flight of steps. On the left the stable yard, with its gateway, encroaches on the garden. There are fruit bushes along the paling and house, covered with washing hung out to dry. A path runs by the house, and rises by two steps at the corner where it turns out of the right along the front. In the middle a small table, with two bent wood chairs at it, is laid for breakfast with Turkish coffee pot, cups, rolls, etc.; but the cups have been used and the bread broken. There is a wooden garden seat against the wall on the left.

Louka, smoking a cigaret, is standing between the table and the house, turning her back with angry disdain on a man-servant who is lecturing her. He is a middle-aged man of cool temperament and low but clear and keen intelligence, with the complacency of the servant who values himself on his rank in servility, and the imperturbability of the accurate calculator who has no illusions. He wears a white Bulgarian costume jacket with decorated harder, sash, wide knickerbockers, and decorated gaiters. His head is shaved up to the crown, giving him a high Japanese forehead. His name is Nicola.

NICOLA. Be warned in time, Louka: mend your manners. I know the mistress. She is so grand that she never dreams that any servant could dare to be disrespectful to her; but if she once suspects that you are defying her, out you go.

LOUKA. I do defy her. I will defy her. What do I care for her?

NICOLA. If you quarrel with the family, I never can marry you. It's the same as if you quarrelled with me!

LOUKA. You take her part against me, do you?

NICOLA (sedately). I shall always be dependent on the good will of the family. When I leave their service and start a shop in Sofia, their custom will be half my capital: their bad word would ruin me.

LOUKA. You have no spirit. I should like to see them dare say a word against me!

NICOLA (pityingly). I should have expected more sense from you, Louka. But you're young, you're young!

LOUKA. Yes; and you like me the better for it, don't you? But I know some family secrets they wouldn't care to have told, young as I am. Let them quarrel with me if they dare!

NICOLA (with compassionate superiority). Do you know what they would do if they heard you talk like that?

LOUKA. What could they do?

NICOLA. Discharge you for untruthfulness. Who would believe any stories you told after that? Who would give you another situation? Who in this house would dare be seen speaking to you ever again? How long would your father be left on his little farm? (She impatiently throws away the end of her cigaret, and stamps on it.) Child, you don't know the power such high people have over the like of you and me when we try to rise out of our poverty against them. (He goes close to her and lowers his voice.) Look at me, ten years in their service. Do you think I know no secrets? I know things about the mistress that she wouldn't have the master know for a thousand levas. I know things about him that she wouldn't let him hear the last of for six months if I blabbed them to her. I know things about Raina that would break off her match with Sergius if—

LOUKA (turning on him quickly). How do you know? I never told you!

NICOLA (opening his eyes cunningly). So that's your little secret, is it? I thought it might be something like that. Well, you take my advice, and be respectful; and make the mistress feel that no matter what you know or don't know, they can depend on you to hold your tongue and serve the family faithfully. That's what they like; and that's how you'll make most out of them.

LOUKA (with searching scorn). You have the soul of a servant, Nicola.

NICOLA (complacently). Yes: that's the secret of success in service.

(A loud knocking with a whip handle on a wooden door, outside on the left, is heard.)

MALE VOICE OUTSIDE. Hollo! Hollo there! Nicola!

LOUKA. Master! back from the war!

NICOLA (quickly). My word for it, Louka, the war's over. Off with you and get some fresh coffee. (He runs out into the stable yard.)

LOUKA (as she puts the coffee pot and the cups upon the tray, and carries it into the house). You'll never put the soul of a servant into me.

(Major Petkoff comes from the stable yard, followed by Nicola. He is a cheerful, excitable, insignificant, unpolished man of about 50, naturally unambitious except as to his income and his importance in local society, but just now greatly pleased with the military rank which the war has thrust on him as a man of consequence in his town. The fever of plucky patriotism which the Servian attack roused in all the Bulgarians has pulled him through the war; but he is obviously glad to be home again.)

PETKOFF (pointing to the table with his whip). Breakfast out here, eh?

NICOLA. Yes, sir. The mistress and Miss Raina have just gone in.

PETKOFF (fitting down and taking a roll). Go in and say I've come; and get me some fresh coffee.

NICOLA. It's coming, sir. (He goes to the house door. Louka, with fresh coffee, a clean cup, and a brandy bottle on her tray meets him.) Have you told the mistress?

LOUKA. Yes: she's coming.

(Nicola goes into the house. Louka brings the coffee to the table.)

PETKOFF. Well, the Servians haven't run away with you, have they?

LOUKA. No, sir.

PETKOFF. That's right. Have you brought me some cognac?

LOUKA (putting the bottle on the table). Here, sir.

PETKOFF. That's right. (He pours some into his coffee.)

(Catherine who has at this early hour made only a very perfunctory toilet, and wears a Bulgarian apron over a once brilliant, but now half worn out red dressing gown, and a colored handkerchief tied over her thick black hair, with Turkish slippers on her bare feet, comes from the house, looking astonishingly handsome and stately under all the circumstances. Louka goes into the house.)

CATHERINE. My dear Paul, what a surprise for us. (She stoops over the back of his chair to kiss him.) Have they brought you fresh coffee?

PETKOFF. Yes, Louka's been looking after me. The war's over. The treaty was signed three days ago at Bucharest; and the decree for our army to demobilize was issued yesterday.

CATHERINE (springing erect, with flashing eyes). The war over! Paul: have you let the Austrians force you to make peace?

PETKOFF (submissively). My dear: they didn't consult me. What could *I* do? (She sits down and turns away from him.) But of course we saw to it that the treaty was an honorable one. It declares peace—

CATHERINE (outraged). Peace!

PETKOFF (appeasing her).—but not friendly relations: remember that. They wanted to put that in; but I insisted on its being struck out. What more could I do?

18

CATHERINE. You could have annexed Servia and made Prince Alexander Emperor of the Balkans. That's what I would have done.

PETKOFF. I don't doubt it in the least, my dear. But I should have had to subdue the whole Austrian Empire first; and that would have kept me too long away from you. I missed you greatly.

CATHERINE (relenting). Ah! (Stretches her hand affectionately across the table to squeeze his.)

PETKOFF. And how have you been, my dear?

CATHERINE. Oh, my usual sore throats, that's all.

PETKOFF (with conviction). That comes from washing your neck every day. I've often told you so.

CATHERINE. Nonsense, Paul!

PETKOFF (over his coffee and cigaret). I don't believe in going too far with these modern customs. All this washing can't be good for the health: it's not natural. There was an Englishman at Phillipopolis who used to wet himself all over with cold water every morning when he got up. Disgusting! It all comes from the English: their climate makes them so dirty that they have to be perpetually washing themselves. Look at my father: he never had a bath in his life; and he lived to be ninety-eight, the healthiest man in Bulgaria. I don't mind a good wash once a week to keep up my position; but once a day is carrying the thing to a ridiculous extreme.

CATHERINE. You are a barbarian at heart still, Paul. I hope you behaved yourself before all those Russian officers.

PETKOFF. I did my best. I took care to let them know that we had a library.

CATHERINE. Ah; but you didn't tell them that we have an electric bell in it? I have had one put up.

PETKOFF. What's an electric bell?

CATHERINE. You touch a button; something tinkles in the kitchen; and then Nicola comes up.

PETKOFF. Why not shout for him?

CATHERINE. Civilized people never shout for their servants. I've learnt that while you were away.

PETKOFF. Well, I'll tell you something I've learnt, too. Civilized people don't hang out their washing to dry where visitors can see it; so you'd better have all that (indicating the clothes on the bushes) put somewhere else.

CATHERINE. Oh, that's absurd, Paul: I don't believe really refined people notice such things.

(Someone is heard knocking at the stable gates.)

PETKOFF. There's Sergius. (Shouting.) Hollo, Nicola!

CATHERINE. Oh, don't shout, Paul: it really isn't nice.

PETKOFF. Bosh! (He shouts louder than before.) Nicola!

NICOLA (appearing at the house door). Yes, sir.

PETKOFF. If that is Major Saranoff, bring him round this way. (He pronounces the name with the stress on the second syllable—Sarah-noff.)

NICOLA. Yes, sir. (He goes into the stable yard.)

PETKOFF. You must talk to him, my dear, until Raina takes him off our hands. He bores my life out about our not promoting him—over my head, mind you.

CATHERINE. He certainly ought to be promoted when he marries Raina. Besides, the country should insist on having at least one native general.

PETKOFF. Yes, so that he could throw away whole brigades instead of regiments. It's no use, my dear: he has not the slightest chance of promotion until we are quite sure that the peace will be a lasting one.

NICOLA (at the gate, announcing). Major Sergius Saranoff! (He goes into the house and returns presently with a third chair, which he places at the table. He then withdraws.)

(Major Sergius Saranoff, the original of the portrait in Raina's room, is a tall, romantically handsome man, with the physical hardihood, the high spirit, and the susceptible imagination of an untamed mountaineer chieftain. But his remarkable personal distinction is of a characteristically civilized type. The ridges of his eyebrows, curving with a ram's-horn twist round the marked projections at the outer corners, his jealously observant eye, his nose, thin, keen, and apprehensive in spite of the pugnacious high bridge and large nostril, his assertive chin, would not be out of place in a Paris salon. In short, the clever, imaginative barbarian has an acute critical faculty which has been thrown into intense activity by the arrival of western civilization in the Balkans; and the result is precisely what the advent of nineteenth-century thought first produced in England: to-wit, Byronism. By his brooding on the perpetual failure, not only of others, but of himself, to live up to his imaginative ideals, his consequent cynical scorn for humanity, the jejune credulity as to the absolute validity of his ideals and the unworthiness of the world in disregarding them, his wincings and mockeries under the sting of the petty disillusions which every hour spent among men brings to his infallibly quick observation, he has acquired the half tragic, half ironic air, the mysterious moodiness, the suggestion of a strange and terrible history that has left him nothing but undying remorse, by which Childe Harold fascinated the grandmothers of his English contemporaries. Altogether it is clear that here or nowhere is Raina's ideal hero. Catherine is hardly less enthusiastic, and much less reserved in shewing her enthusiasm. As he enters from the stable gate, she rises effusively to greet him. Petkoff is distinctly less disposed to make a fuss about him.)

PETKOFF. Here already, Sergius. Glad to see you!

CATHERINE. My dear Sergius!(She holds out both her hands.)

SERGIUS (kissing them with scrupulous gallantry). My dear mother, if I may call you so.

PETKOFF (drily). Mother-in-law, Sergius; mother-in-law! Sit down, and have some coffee.

SERGIUS. Thank you, none for me. (He gets away from the table with a certain distaste for Petkoff's enjoyment of it, and posts himself with conscious grace against the rail of the steps leading to the house.)

CATHERINE. You look superb—splendid. The campaign has improved you. Everybody here is mad about you. We were all wild with enthusiasm about that magnificent cavalry charge.

SERGIUS (with grave irony). Madam: it was the cradle and the grave of my military reputation.

CATHERINE. How so?

SERGIUS. I won the battle the wrong way when our worthy Russian generals were losing it the right way. That upset their plans, and wounded their self-esteem. Two of their colonels got their regiments driven back on the correct principles of scientific warfare. Two major-generals got killed strictly according to military etiquette. Those two colonels are now major-generals; and I am still a simple major.

CATHERINE. You shall not remain so, Sergius. The women are on your side; and they will see that justice is done you.

SERGIUS. It is too late. I have only waited for the peace to send in my resignation.

PETKOFF (dropping his cup in his amazement). Your resignation!

CATHERINE. Oh, you must withdraw it!

SERGIUS (with resolute, measured emphasis, folding his arms). I never withdraw!

PETKOFF (vexed). Now who could have supposed you were going to do such a thing?

SERGIUS (with fire). Everyone that knew me. But enough of myself and my affairs. How is Raina; and where is Raina?

RAINA (suddenly coming round the corner of the house and standing at the top of the steps in the path). Raina is here. (She makes a charming picture as they all turn to look at her. She wears an underdress of pale green silk, draped with an overdress of thin ecru canvas embroidered with gold. On her head she wears a pretty Phrygian cap of gold tinsel. Sergius, with an exclamation of pleasure, goes impulsively to meet her. She stretches out her hand: he drops chivalrously on one knee and kisses it.)

PETKOFF (aside to Catherine, beaming with parental pride). Pretty, isn't it? She always appears at the right moment.

CATHERINE (impatiently). Yes: she listens for it. It is an abominable habit.

(Sergius leads Raina forward with splendid gallantry, as if she were a queen. When they come to the table, she turns to him with a bend of the head; he bows; and thus they separate, he coming to his place, and she going behind her father's chair.)

RAINA (stooping and kissing her father). Dear father! Welcome home!

PETKOFF (patting her cheek). My little pet girl. (He kisses her; she goes to the chair left by Nicola for Sergius, and sits down.)

CATHERINE. And so you're no longer a soldier, Sergius.

SERGIUS. I am no longer a soldier. Soldiering, my dear madam, is the coward's art of attacking mercilessly when you are strong, and keeping out of harm's way when you are weak. That is the whole secret of successful fighting. Get your enemy at a disadvantage; and never, on any account, fight him on equal terms. Eh, Major!

PETKOFF. They wouldn't let us make a fair stand-up fight of it. However, I suppose soldiering has to be a trade like any other trade.

SERGIUS. Precisely. But I have no ambition to succeed as a tradesman; so I have taken the advice of that bagman of a captain that settled the exchange of prisoners with us at Peerot, and given it up.

PETKOFF. What, that Swiss fellow? Sergius: I've often thought of that exchange since. He over-reached us about those horses.

SERGIUS. Of course he over-reached us. His father was a hotel and livery stable keeper; and he owed his first step to his knowledge of horse-dealing. (With mock enthusiasm.) Ah, he was a soldier—every inch a soldier! If only I had bought the horses for my regiment instead of foolishly leading it into danger, I should have been a field-marshal now!

CATHERINE. A Swiss? What was he doing in the Servian army?

PETKOFF. A volunteer of course—keen on picking up his profession. (Chuckling.) We shouldn't have been able to begin fighting if these foreigners hadn't shewn us how to do it: we knew nothing about it; and neither did the Servians. Egad, there'd have been no war without them.

RAINA. Are there many Swiss officers in the Servian Army?

PETKOFF. No—all Austrians, just as our officers were all Russians. This was the only Swiss I came across. I'll never trust a Swiss again. He cheated us—humbugged us into giving him fifty able bodied men for two hundred confounded worn out chargers. They weren't even eatable!

SERGIUS. We were two children in the hands of that consummate soldier, Major: simply two innocent little children.

RAINA. What was he like?

CATHERINE. Oh, Raina, what a silly question!

SERGIUS. He was like a commercial traveller in uniform. Bourgeois to his boots.

PETKOFF (grinning). Sergius: tell Catherine that queer story his friend told us about him—how he escaped after Slivnitza. You remember?—about his being hid by two women.

SERGIUS (with bitter irony). Oh, yes, quite a romance. He was serving in the very battery I so unprofessionally charged. Being a thorough soldier, he ran away like the rest of them, with our cavalry at his heels. To escape their attentions, he had the good taste to take refuge in the chamber of some patriotic young Bulgarian lady. The young lady was enchanted by his persuasive commercial traveller's manners. She very modestly entertained him for an hour or so and then called in her mother lest her conduct should appear unmaidenly. The old lady was equally fascinated; and the fugitive was sent on his way in the morning, disguised in an old coat belonging to the master of the house, who was away at the war.

RAINA (rising with marked stateliness). Your life in the camp has made you coarse, Sergius. I did not think you would have repeated such a story before me. (She turns away coldly.)

CATHERINE (also rising). She is right, Sergius. If such women exist, we should be spared the knowledge of them.

PETKOFF. Pooh! nonsense! what does it matter?

SERGIUS (ashamed). No, Petkoff: I was wrong. (To Raina, with earnest humility.) I beg your pardon. I have behaved abominably. Forgive me, Raina. (She bows reservedly.) And you, too, madam. (Catherine bows graciously and sits down. He proceeds solemnly, again addressing Raina.) The glimpses I have had of the seamy side of life during the last few months have made me cynical; but I should not have brought my cynicism here—least of all into your presence, Raina. I—(Here, turning to the others, he is evidently about to begin a long speech when the Major interrupts him.)

PETKOFF. Stuff and nonsense, Sergius. That's quite enough fuss about nothing: a soldier's daughter should be able to stand up without flinching to a little strong conversation. (He rises.) Come: it's time for us to get to business. We have to make up our minds how those three regiments are to get back to Phillipopolis:—there's no forage for them on the Sofia route. (He goes towards the house.) Come along. (Sergius is about to follow him when Catherine rises and intervenes.)

CATHERINE. Oh, Paul, can't you spare Sergius for a few moments? Raina has hardly seen him yet. Perhaps I can help you to settle about the regiments.

SERGIUS (protesting). My dear madam, impossible: you—

CATHERINE (stopping him playfully). You stay here, my dear Sergius: there's no hurry. I have a word or two to say to Paul. (Sergius instantly bows and steps back.) Now, dear (taking Petkoff's arm), come and see the electric bell.

PETKOFF. Oh, very well, very well. (They go into the house together affectionately. Sergius, left alone with Raina, looks anxiously at her, fearing that she may be still offended. She smiles, and stretches out her arms to him.)

(Exit R. into house, followed by Catherine.)

SERGIUS (hastening to her, but refraining from touching her without express permission). Am I forgiven?

RAINA (placing her hands on his shoulder as she looks up at him with admiration and worship). My hero! My king.

SERGIUS. My queen! (He kisses her on the forehead with holy awe.)

RAINA. How I have envied you, Sergius! You have been out in the world, on the field of battle, able to prove yourself there worthy of any woman in the world; whilst I have had to sit at home inactive,—dreaming—useless—doing nothing that could give me the right to call myself worthy of any man.

SERGIUS. Dearest, all my deeds have been yours. You inspired me. I have gone through the war like a knight in a tournament with his lady looking on at him!

24

RAINA. And you have never been absent from my thoughts for a moment. (Very solemnly.) Sergius: I think we two have found the higher love. When I think of you, I feel that I could never do a base deed, or think an ignoble thought.

SERGIUS. My lady, and my saint! (Clasping her reverently.)

RAINA (returning his embrace). My lord and my g—

SERGIUS. Sh—sh! Let me be the worshipper, dear. You little know how unworthy even the best man is of a girl's pure passion!

RAINA. I trust you. I love you. You will never disappoint me, Sergius. (Louka is heard singing within the house. They quickly release each other.) Hush! I can't pretend to talk indifferently before her: my heart is too full. (Louka comes from the house with her tray. She goes to the table, and begins to clear it, with her back turned to them.) I will go and get my hat; and then we can go out until lunch time. Wouldn't you like that?

SERGIUS. Be quick. If you are away five minutes, it will seem five hours. (Raina runs to the top of the steps and turns there to exchange a look with him and wave him a kiss with both hands. He looks after her with emotion for a moment, then turns slowly away, his face radiant with the exultation of the scene which has just passed. The movement shifts his field of vision, into the corner of which there now comes the tail of Louka's double apron. His eye gleams at once. He takes a stealthy look at her, and begins to twirl his moustache nervously, with his left hand akimbo on his hip. Finally, striking the ground with his heels in something of a cavalry swagger, he strolls over to the left of the table, opposite her, and says) Louka: do you know what the higher love is?

LOUKA (astonished). No, sir.

SERGIUS. Very fatiguing thing to keep up for any length of time, Louka. One feels the need of some relief after it.

LOUKA (innocently). Perhaps you would like some coffee, sir? (She stretches her hand across the table for the coffee pot.)

SERGIUS (taking her hand). Thank you, Louka.

LOUKA (pretending to pull). Oh, sir, you know I didn't mean that. I'm surprised at you!

SERGIUS (coming clear of the table and drawing her with him). I am surprised at myself, Louka. What would Sergius, the hero of Slivnitza, say if he saw me now? What would Sergius, the apostle of the higher love, say if he saw me now? What would the half dozen Sergiuses who keep popping in and out of this handsome figure of mine say if they caught us here? (Letting go her hand and slipping his arm dexterously round her waist.) Do you consider my figure handsome, Louka?

LOUKA. Let me go, sir. I shall be disgraced. (She struggles: he holds her inexorably.) Oh, will you let go?

SERGIUS (looking straight into her eyes). No.

LOUKA. Then stand back where we can't be seen. Have you no common sense?

SERGIUS. Ah, that's reasonable. (He takes her into the stableyard gateway, where they are hidden from the house.)

LOUKA (complaining). I may have been seen from the windows: Miss Raina is sure to be spying about after you.

SERGIUS (stung—letting her go). Take care, Louka. I may be worthless enough to betray the higher love; but do not you insult it.

LOUKA (demurely). Not for the world, sir, I'm sure. May I go on with my work please, now?

SERGIUS (again putting his arm round her). You are a provoking little witch, Louka. If you were in love with me, would you spy out of windows on me?

LOUKA. Well, you see, sir, since you say you are half a dozen different gentlemen all at once, I should have a great deal to look after.

SERGIUS (charmed). Witty as well as pretty. (He tries to kiss her.)

LOUKA (avoiding him). No, I don't want your kisses. Gentlefolk are all alike—you making love to me behind Miss Raina's back, and she doing the same behind yours.

SERGIUS (recoiling a step). Louka!

LOUKA. It shews how little you really care!

SERGIUS (dropping his familiarity and speaking with freezing politeness). If our conversation is to continue, Louka, you will please remember that a gentleman does not discuss the conduct of the lady he is engaged to with her maid.

LOUKA. It's so hard to know what a gentleman considers right. I thought from your trying to kiss me that you had given up being so particular.

SERGIUS (turning from her and striking his forehead as he comes back into the garden from the gateway). Devil! devil!

LOUKA. Ha! ha! I expect one of the six of you is very like me, sir, though I am only Miss Raina's maid. (She goes back to her work at the table, taking no further notice of him.)

SERGIUS (speaking to himself). Which of the six is the real man?—that's the question that torments me. One of them is a hero, another a buffoon, another a humbug, another perhaps a bit of a blackguard. (He pauses and looks furtively at Louka, as he adds with deep bitterness) And one, at least, is a coward—jealous, like all cowards. (He goes to the table.) Louka.

LOUKA. Yes?

SERGIUS. Who is my rival?

LOUKA. You shall never get that out of me, for love or money.

SERGIUS. Why?

LOUKA. Never mind why. Besides, you would tell that I told you; and I should lose my place.

SERGIUS (holding out his right hand in affirmation). No; on the honor of a—(He checks himself, and his hand drops nerveless as he concludes, sardonically)—of a man capable of behaving as I have been behaving for the last five minutes. Who is he?

LOUKA. I don't know. I never saw him. I only heard his voice through the door of her room.

SERGIUS. Damnation! How dare you?

LOUKA (retreating). Oh, I mean no harm: you've no right to take up my words like that. The mistress knows all about it. And I tell you that if that gentleman ever comes here again, Miss Raina will marry him, whether he likes it or not. I know the difference between the sort of manner you and she put on before one another and the real manner. (Sergius shivers as if she had stabbed him. Then, setting his face like iron, he strides grimly to her, and grips her above the elbows with both bands.)

SERGIUS. Now listen you to me!

LOUKA (wincing). Not so tight: you're hurting me!

SERGIUS. That doesn't matter. You have stained my honor by making me a party to your eavesdropping. And you have betrayed your mistress—

LOUKA (writhing). Please—

SERGIUS. That shews that you are an abominable little clod of common clay, with the soul of a servant. (He lets her go as if she were an unclean thing, and turns away, dusting his hands of her, to the bench by the wall, where he sits down with averted head, meditating gloomily.)

LOUKA (whimpering angrily with her hands up her sleeves, feeling her bruised arms). You know how to hurt with your tongue as well as with your hands. But I don't care, now I've found out that whatever clay I'm made of, you're made of the same. As for her, she's a liar; and her fine airs are a cheat; and I'm worth six of her. (She shakes the pain off hardily; tosses her head; and sets to work to put the things on the tray. He looks doubtfully at her once or twice. She finishes packing the tray, and laps the cloth over the edges, so as to carry all out together. As she stoops to lift it, he rises.)

SERGIUS. Louka! (She stops and looks defiantly at him with the tray in her hands.) A gentleman has no right to hurt a woman under any circumstances. (With profound humility, uncovering his head.) I beg your pardon.

LOUKA. That sort of apology may satisfy a lady. Of what use is it to a servant?

SERGIUS (thus rudely crossed in his chivalry, throws it off with a bitter laugh and says slightingly). Oh, you wish to be paid for the hurt? (He puts on his shako, and takes some money from his pocket.)

LOUKA (her eyes filling with tears in spite of herself). No, I want my hurt made well.

SERGIUS (sobered by her tone). How?

(She rolls up her left sleeve; clasps her arm with the thumb and fingers of her right hand; and looks down at the bruise. Then she raises her head and looks straight at him. Finally, with a superb gesture she presents her arm to be kissed. Amazed, he looks at her; at the arm; at her again; hesitates; and then, with shuddering intensity, exclaims)

SERGIUS. Never! (and gets away as far as possible from her.)

(Her arm drops. Without a word, and with unaffected dignity, she takes her tray, and is approaching the house when Raina returns wearing a hat and jacket in the height of the Vienna fashion of the previous year, 1885. Louka makes way proudly for her, and then goes into the house.)

RAINA. I'm ready! What's the matter? (Gaily.) Have you been flirting with Louka?

SERGIUS (hastily). No, no. How can you think such a thing?

RAINA (ashamed of herself). Forgive me, dear: it was only a jest. I am so happy to-day.

(He goes quickly to her, and kisses her hand remorsefully. Catherine comes out and calls to them from the top of the steps.)

CATHERINE (coming down to them). I am sorry to disturb you, children; but Paul is distracted over those three regiments. He does not know how to get them to Phillipopolis;

28

and he objects to every suggestion of mine. You must go and help him, Sergius. He is in the library.

RAINA (disappointed). But we are just going out for a walk.

SERGIUS. I shall not be long. Wait for me just five minutes. (He runs up the steps to the door.)

RAINA (following him to the foot of the steps and looking up at him with timid coquetry). I shall go round and wait in full view of the library windows. Be sure you draw father's attention to me. If you are a moment longer than five minutes, I shall go in and fetch you, regiments or no regiments.

SERGIUS (laughing). Very well. (He goes in. Raina watches him until he is out of her sight. Then, with a perceptible relaxation of manner, she begins to pace up and down about the garden in a brown study.)

CATHERINE. Imagine their meeting that Swiss and hearing the whole story! The very first thing your father asked for was the old coat we sent him off in. A nice mess you have got us into!

RAINA (gazing thoughtfully at the gravel as she walks). The little beast!

CATHERINE. Little beast! What little beast?

RAINA. To go and tell! Oh, if I had him here, I'd stuff him with chocolate creams till he couldn't ever speak again!

CATHERINE. Don't talk nonsense. Tell me the truth, Raina. How long was he in your room before you came to me?

RAINA (whisking round and recommencing her march in the opposite direction). Oh, I forget.

CATHERINE. You cannot forget! Did he really climb up after the soldiers were gone, or was he there when that officer searched the room?

RAINA. No. Yes, I think he must have been there then.

CATHERINE. You think! Oh, Raina, Raina! Will anything ever make you straightforward? If Sergius finds out, it is all over between you.

RAINA (with cool impertinence). Oh, I know Sergius is your pet. I sometimes wish you could marry him instead of me. You would just suit him. You would pet him, and spoil him, and mother him to perfection.

CATHERINE (opening her eyes very widely indeed). Well, upon my word!

RAINA (capriciously—half to herself). I always feel a longing to do or say something dreadful to him—to shock his propriety—to scandalize the five senses out of him! (To Catherine perversely.) I don't care whether he finds out about the chocolate cream soldier or not. I half hope he may. (She again turns flippantly away and strolls up the path to the corner of the house.)

CATHERINE. And what should I be able to say to your father, pray?

RAINA (over her shoulder, from the top of the two steps). Oh, poor father! As if he could help himself! (She turns the corner and passes out of sight.)

CATHERINE (looking after her, her fingers itching). Oh, if you were only ten years younger! (Louka comes from the house with a salver, which she carries hanging down by her side.) Well?

LOUKA. There's a gentleman just called, madam—a Servian officer—

CATHERINE (flaming). A Servian! How dare he—(Checking herself bitterly.) Oh, I forgot. We are at peace now. I suppose we shall have them calling every day to pay their compliments. Well, if he is an officer why don't you tell your master? He is in the library with Major Saranoff. Why do you come to me?

LOUKA. But he asks for you, madam. And I don't think he knows who you are: he said the lady of the house. He gave me this little ticket for you. (She takes a card out of her bosom; puts it on the salver and offers it to Catherine.)

CATHERINE (reading). "Captain Bluntschli!" That's a German name.

LOUKA. Swiss, madam, I think.

CATHERINE (with a bound that makes Louka jump back). Swiss! What is he like?

LOUKA (timidly). He has a big carpet bag, madam.

CATHERINE. Oh, Heavens, he's come to return the coat! Send him away—say we're not at home—ask him to leave his address and I'll write to him—Oh, stop: that will never do. Wait! (She throws herself into a chair to think it out. Louka waits.) The master and Major Saranoff are busy in the library, aren't they?

LOUKA. Yes, madam.

CATHERINE (decisively). Bring the gentleman out here at once. (Imperatively.) And be very polite to him. Don't delay. Here (impatiently snatching the salver from her): leave that here; and go straight back to him.

LOUKA. Yes, madam. (Going.)

CATHERINE. Louka!

LOUKA (stopping). Yes, madam.

CATHERINE. Is the library door shut?

LOUKA. I think so, madam.

CATHERINE. If not, shut it as you pass through.

LOUKA. Yes, madam. (Going.)

CATHERINE. Stop! (Louka stops.) He will have to go out that way (indicating the gate of the stable yard). Tell Nicola to bring his bag here after him. Don't forget.

LOUKA (surprised). His bag?

CATHERINE. Yes, here, as soon as possible. (Vehemently.) Be quick! (Louka runs into the house. Catherine snatches her apron off and throws it behind a bush. She then takes up the salver and uses it as a mirror, with the result that the handkerchief tied round her head follows the apron. A touch to her hair and a shake to her dressing gown makes her presentable.) Oh, how—how—how can a man be such a fool! Such a moment to select! (Louka appears at the door of the house, announcing "Captain Bluntschli;" and standing aside at the top of the steps to let him pass before she goes in again. He is the man of the adventure in Raina's room. He is now clean, well brushed, smartly uniformed, and out of trouble, but still unmistakably the same man. The moment Louka's back is turned, Catherine swoops on him with hurried, urgent, coaxing appeal.) Captain Bluntschli, I am very glad to see you; but you must leave this house at once. (He raises his eyebrows.) My husband has just returned, with my future son-in-law; and they know nothing. If they did, the consequences would be terrible. You are a foreigner: you do not feel our national animosities as we do. We still hate the Servians: the only effect of the peace on my husband is to make him feel like a lion baulked of his prey. If he discovered our secret, he would never forgive me; and my daughter's life would hardly be safe. Will you, like the chivalrous gentleman and soldier you are, leave at once before he finds you here?

BLUNTSCHLI (disappointed, but philosophical). At once, gracious lady. I only came to thank you and return the coat you lent me. If you will allow me to take it out of my bag and leave it with your servant as I pass out, I need detain you no further. (He turns to go into the house.)

CATHERINE (catching him by the sleeve). Oh, you must not think of going back that way. (Coaxing him across to the stable gates.) This is the shortest way out. Many thanks. So glad to have been of service to you. Good-bye.

BLUNTSCHLI. But my bag?

CATHERINE. It will be sent on. You will leave me your address.

BLUNTSCHLI. True. Allow me. (He takes out his card-case, and stops to write his address, keeping Catherine in an agony of impatience. As he hands her the card, Petkoff, hatless, rushes from the house in a fluster of hospitality, followed by Sergius.)

PETKOFF (as he hurries down the steps). My dear Captain Bluntschli—

CATHERINE. Oh Heavens! (She sinks on the seat against the wall.)

PETKOFF (too preoccupied to notice her as he shakes Bluntschli's hand heartily). Those stupid people of mine thought I was out here, instead of in the—haw!—library. (He cannot mention the library without betraying how proud he is of it.) I saw you through the window. I was wondering why you didn't come in. Saranoff is with me: you remember him, don't you?

SERGIUS (saluting humorously, and then offering his hand with great charm of manner). Welcome, our friend the enemy!

PETKOFF. No longer the enemy, happily. (Rather anxiously.) I hope you've come as a friend, and not on business.

CATHERINE. Oh, quite as a friend, Paul. I was just asking Captain Bluntschli to stay to lunch; but he declares he must go at once.

SERGIUS (sardonically). Impossible, Bluntschli. We want you here badly. We have to send on three cavalry regiments to Phillipopolis; and we don't in the least know how to do it.

BLUNTSCHLI (suddenly attentive and business-like). Phillipopolis! The forage is the trouble, eh?

PETKOFF (eagerly). Yes, that's it. (To Sergius.) He sees the whole thing at once.

BLUNTSCHLI. I think I can shew you how to manage that.

SERGIUS. Invaluable man! Come along! (Towering over Bluntschli, he puts his hand on his shoulder and takes him to the steps, Petkoff following. As Bluntschli puts his foot on the first step, Raina comes out of the house.)

RAINA (completely losing her presence of mind). Oh, the chocolate cream soldier!

(Bluntschli stands rigid. Sergius, amazed, looks at Raina, then at Petkoff, who looks back at him and then at his wife.)

CATHERINE (with commanding presence of mind). My dear Raina, don't you see that we have a guest here—Captain Bluntschli, one of our new Servian friends?

(Raina bows; Bluntschli bows.)

RAINA. How silly of me! (She comes down into the centre of the group, between Bluntschli and Petkoff) I made a beautiful ornament this morning for the ice pudding; and that stupid Nicola has just put down a pile of plates on it and spoiled it. (To Bluntschli, winningly.) I hope you didn't think that you were the chocolate cream soldier, Captain Bluntschli.

BLUNTSCHLI (laughing). I assure you I did. (Stealing a whimsical glance at her.) Your explanation was a relief.

PETKOFF (suspiciously, to Raina). And since when, pray, have you taken to cooking?

CATHERINE. Oh, whilst you were away. It is her latest fancy.

PETKOFF (testily). And has Nicola taken to drinking? He used to be careful enough. First he shews Captain Bluntschli out here when he knew quite well I was in the—hum!—library; and then he goes downstairs and breaks Raina's chocolate soldier. He must—(At this moment Nicola appears at the top of the steps R., with a carpet bag. He descends; places it respectfully before Bluntschli; and waits for further orders. General amazement. Nicola, unconscious of the effect he is producing, looks perfectly satisfied with himself. When Petkoff recovers his power of speech, he breaks out at him with) Are you mad, Nicola?

NICOLA (taken aback). Sir?

PETKOFF. What have you brought that for?

NICOLA. My lady's orders, sir. Louka told me that—

CATHERINE (interrupting him). My orders! Why should I order you to bring Captain Bluntschli's luggage out here? What are you thinking of, Nicola?

NICOLA (after a moment's bewilderment, picking up the bag as he addresses Bluntschli with the very perfection of servile discretion). I beg your pardon, sir, I am sure. (To Catherine.) My fault, madam! I hope you'll overlook it! (He bows, and is going to the steps with the bag, when Petkoff addresses him angrily.)

PETKOFF. You'd better go and slam that bag, too, down on Miss Raina's ice pudding! (This is too much for Nicola. The bag drops from his hands on Petkoff's corns, eliciting a roar of anguish from him.) Begone, you butter-fingered donkey.

NICOLA (snatching up the bag, and escaping into the house). Yes, sir.

CATHERINE. Oh, never mind, Paul, don't be angry!

PETKOFF (muttering). Scoundrel. He's got out of hand while I was away. I'll teach him. (Recollecting his guest.) Oh, well, never mind. Come, Bluntschli, lets have no more nonsense about you having to go away. You know very well you're not going back to Switzerland yet. Until you do go back you'll stay with us.

RAINA. Oh, do, Captain Bluntschli.

PETKOFF (to Catherine). Now, Catherine, it's of you that he's afraid. Press him and he'll stay.

CATHERINE. Of course I shall be only too delighted if (appealingly) Captain Bluntschli really wishes to stay. He knows my wishes.

BLUNTSCHLI (in his driest military manner). I am at madame's orders.

SERGIUS (cordially). That settles it!

PETKOFF (heartily). Of course!

RAINA. You see, you must stay!

BLUNTSCHLI (smiling). Well, If I must, I must! (Gesture of despair from Catherine.)

ACT III

In the library after lunch. It is not much of a library, its literary equipment consisting of a single fixed shelf stocked with old paper-covered novels, broken backed, coffee stained, torn and thumbed, and a couple of little hanging shelves with a few gift books on them, the rest of the wall space being occupied by trophies of war and the chase. But it is a most comfortable sitting-room. A row of three large windows in the front of the house shew a mountain panorama, which is just now seen in one of its softest aspects in the mellowing afternoon light. In the left hand corner, a square earthenware stove, a perfect tower of colored pottery, rises nearly to the ceiling and guarantees plenty of warmth. The ottoman in the middle is a circular bank of decorated cushions, and the window seats are well upholstered divans. Little Turkish tables, one of them with an elaborate hookah on it, and a screen to match them, complete the handsome effect of the furnishing. There is one object, however, which is hopelessly out of keeping with its surroundings. This is a small kitchen table, much the worse for wear, fitted as a writing table with an old canister full of pens, an eggcup filled with ink, and a deplorable scrap of severely used pink blotting paper.

At the side of this table, which stands on the right, Bluntschli is hard at work, with a couple of maps before him, writing orders. At the head of it sits Sergius, who is also supposed to be at work, but who is actually gnawing the feather of a pen, and contemplating Bluntschli's quick, sure, businesslike progress with a mixture of envious irritation at his own incapacity, and awestruck wonder at an ability which seems to him almost miraculous, though its prosaic character forbids him to esteem it. The major is comfortably established on the ottoman, with a newspaper in his hand and the tube of the hookah within his reach. Catherine sits at the stove, with her back to them, embroidering. Raina, reclining on the divan under the left hand window, is gazing in a daydream out at the Balkan landscape, with a neglected novel in her lap.

The door is on the left. The button of the electric bell is between the door and the fireplace.

PETKOFF (looking up from his paper to watch how they are getting on at the table). Are you sure I can't help you in any way, Bluntschli?

BLUNTSCHLI (without interrupting his writing or looking up). Quite sure, thank you. Saranoff and I will manage it.

SERGIUS (grimly). Yes: we'll manage it. He finds out what to do; draws up the orders; and I sign 'em. Division of labour, Major. (Bluntschli passes him a paper.) Another one? Thank you. (He plants the papers squarely before him; sets his chair carefully parallel to them; and signs with the air of a man resolutely performing a difficult and dangerous feat.) This hand is more accustomed to the sword than to the pen.

PETKOFF. It's very good of you, Bluntschli, it is indeed, to let yourself be put upon in this way. Now are you quite sure I can do nothing?

CATHERINE (in a low, warning tone). You can stop interrupting, Paul.

PETKOFF (starting and looking round at her). Eh? Oh! Quite right, my love, quite right. (He takes his newspaper up, but lets it drop again.) Ah, you haven't been campaigning, Catherine: you don't know how pleasant it is for us to sit here, after a good lunch, with nothing to do but enjoy ourselves. There's only one thing I want to make me thoroughly comfortable.

CATHERINE. What is that?

PETKOFF. My old coat. I'm not at home in this one: I feel as if I were on parade.

CATHERINE. My dear Paul, how absurd you are about that old coat! It must be hanging in the blue closet where you left it.

PETKOFF. My dear Catherine, I tell you I've looked there. Am I to believe my own eyes or not? (Catherine quietly rises and presses the button of the electric bell by the fireplace.) What are you shewing off that bell for? (She looks at him majestically, and silently resumes her chair and her needlework.) My dear: if you think the obstinacy of your sex can make a coat out of two old dressing gowns of Raina's, your waterproof, and my mackintosh, you're mistaken. That's exactly what the blue closet contains at present. (Nicola presents himself.)

CATHERINE (unmoved by Petkoff's sally). Nicola: go to the blue closet and bring your master's old coat here—the braided one he usually wears in the house.

NICOLA. Yes, madam. (Nicola goes out.)

PETKOFF. Catherine.

CATHERINE. Yes, Paul?

PETKOFF. I bet you any piece of jewellery you like to order from Sofia against a week's housekeeping money, that the coat isn't there.

CATHERINE. Done, Paul.

PETKOFF (excited by the prospect of a gamble). Come: here's an opportunity for some sport. Who'll bet on it? Bluntschli: I'll give you six to one.

BLUNTSCHLI (imperturbably). It would be robbing you, Major. Madame is sure to be right. (Without looking up, he passes another batch of papers to Sergius.)

SERGIUS (also excited). Bravo, Switzerland! Major: I bet my best charger against an Arab mare for Raina that Nicola finds the coat in the blue closet.

PETKOFF (eagerly). Your best char—

CATHERINE (hastily interrupting him). Don't be foolish, Paul. An Arabian mare will cost you 50,000 levas.

RAINA (suddenly coming out of her picturesque revery). Really, mother, if you are going to take the jewellery, I don't see why you should grudge me my Arab.

(Nicola comes back with the coat and brings it to Petkoff, who can hardly believe his eyes.)

CATHERINE. Where was it, Nicola?

NICOLA. Hanging in the blue closet, madam.

PETKOFF. Well, I am d—

CATHERINE (stopping him). Paul!

PETKOFF. I could have sworn it wasn't there. Age is beginning to tell on me. I'm getting hallucinations. (To Nicola.) Here: help me to change. Excuse me, Bluntschli. (He begins changing coats, Nicola acting as valet.) Remember: I didn't take that bet of yours, Sergius. You'd better give Raina that Arab steed yourself, since you've roused her expectations. Eh, Raina? (He looks round at her; but she is again rapt in the landscape. With a little gush of paternal affection and pride, he points her out to them and says) She's dreaming, as usual.

SERGIUS. Assuredly she shall not be the loser.

PETKOFF. So much the better for her. I shan't come off so cheap, I expect. (The change is now complete. Nicola goes out with the discarded coat.) Ah, now I feel at home at last. (He sits down and takes his newspaper with a grunt of relief.)

BLUNTSCHLI (to Sergius, handing a paper). That's the last order.

PETKOFF (jumping up). What! finished?

BLUNTSCHLI. Finished. (Petkoff goes beside Sergius; looks curiously over his left shoulder as he signs; and says with childlike envy) Haven't you anything for me to sign?

BLUNTSCHLI. Not necessary. His signature will do.

PETKOFF. Ah, well, I think we've done a thundering good day's work. (He goes away from the table.) Can I do anything more?

BLUNTSCHLI. You had better both see the fellows that are to take these. (To Sergius.) Pack them off at once; and shew them that I've marked on the orders the time they should hand them in by. Tell them that if they stop to drink or tell stories—if they're five minutes late, they'll have the skin taken off their backs.

SERGIUS (rising indignantly). I'll say so. And if one of them is man enough to spit in my face for insulting him, I'll buy his discharge and give him a pension. (He strides out, his humanity deeply outraged.)

BLUNTSCHLI (confidentially). Just see that he talks to them properly, Major, will you?

PETKOFF (officiously). Quite right, Bluntschli, quite right. I'll see to it. (He goes to the door importantly, but hesitates on the threshold.) By the bye, Catherine, you may as well come, too. They'll be far more frightened of you than of me.

CATHERINE (putting down her embroidery). I daresay I had better. You will only splutter at them. (She goes out, Petkoff holding the door for her and following her.)

BLUNTSCHLI. What a country! They make cannons out of cherry trees; and the officers send for their wives to keep discipline! (He begins to fold and docket the papers. Raina, who has risen from the divan, strolls down the room with her hands clasped behind her, and looks mischievously at him.)

RAINA. You look ever so much nicer than when we last met. (He looks up, surprised.) What have you done to yourself?

BLUNTSCHLI. Washed; brushed; good night's sleep and breakfast. That's all.

RAINA. Did you get back safely that morning?

BLUNTSCHLI. Quite, thanks.

RAINA. Were they angry with you for running away from Sergius's charge?

BLUNTSCHLI. No, they were glad; because they'd all just run away themselves.

RAINA (going to the table, and leaning over it towards him). It must have made a lovely story for them—all that about me and my room.

BLUNTSCHLI. Capital story. But I only told it to one of them—a particular friend.

RAINA. On whose discretion you could absolutely rely?

BLUNTSCHLI. Absolutely.

RAINA. Hm! He told it all to my father and Sergius the day you exchanged the prisoners. (She turns away and strolls carelessly across to the other side of the room.)

BLUNTSCHLI (deeply concerned and half incredulous). No! you don't mean that, do you?

RAINA (turning, with sudden earnestness). I do indeed. But they don't know that it was in this house that you hid. If Sergius knew, he would challenge you and kill you in a duel.

BLUNTSCHLI. Bless me! then don't tell him.

RAINA (full of reproach for his levity). Can you realize what it is to me to deceive him? I want to be quite perfect with Sergius—no meanness, no smallness, no deceit. My relation to him is the one really beautiful and noble part of my life. I hope you can understand that.

BLUNTSCHLI (sceptically). You mean that you wouldn't like him to find out that the story about the ice pudding was a—a—a—You know.

RAINA (wincing). Ah, don't talk of it in that flippant way. I lied: I know it. But I did it to save your life. He would have killed you. That was the second time I ever uttered a falsehood. (Bluntschli rises quickly and looks doubtfully and somewhat severely at her.) Do you remember the first time?

BLUNTSCHLI. I! No. Was I present?

RAINA. Yes; and I told the officer who was searching for you that you were not present.

BLUNTSCHLI. True. I should have remembered it.

RAINA (greatly encouraged). Ah, it is natural that you should forget it first. It cost you nothing: it cost me a lie!—a lie!! (She sits down on the ottoman, looking straight before her with her hands clasped on her knee. Bluntschli, quite touched, goes to the ottoman with a particularly reassuring and considerate air, and sits down beside her.)

BLUNTSCHLI. My dear young lady, don't let this worry you. Remember: I'm a soldier. Now what are the two things that happen to a soldier so often that he comes to think nothing of them? One is hearing people tell lies (Raina recoils): the other is getting his life saved in all sorts of ways by all sorts of people.

RAINA (rising in indignant protest). And so he becomes a creature incapable of faith and of gratitude.

BLUNTSCHLI (making a wry face). Do you like gratitude? I don't. If pity is akin to love, gratitude is akin to the other thing.

RAINA. Gratitude! (Turning on him.) If you are incapable of gratitude you are incapable of any noble sentiment. Even animals are grateful. Oh, I see now exactly what you think of me! You were not surprised to hear me lie. To you it was something I probably did every day— every hour. That is how men think of women. (She walks up the room melodramatically.)

BLUNTSCHLI (dubiously). There's reason in everything. You said you'd told only two lies in your whole life. Dear young lady: isn't that rather a short allowance? I'm quite a straightforward man myself; but it wouldn't last me a whole morning.

RAINA (staring haughtily at him). Do you know, sir, that you are insulting me?

BLUNTSCHLI. I can't help it. When you get into that noble attitude and speak in that thrilling voice, I admire you; but I find it impossible to believe a single word you say.

RAINA (superbly). Captain Bluntschli!

BLUNTSCHLI (unmoved). Yes?

RAINA (coming a little towards him, as if she could not believe her senses). Do you mean what you said just now? Do you know what you said just now?

BLUNTSCHLI. I do.

RAINA (gasping). I! I! I!!! (She points to herself incredulously, meaning "I, Raina Petkoff, tell lies!" He meets her gaze unflinchingly. She suddenly sits down beside him, and adds, with a complete change of manner from the heroic to the familiar) How did you find me out?

BLUNTSCHLI (promptly). Instinct, dear young lady. Instinct, and experience of the world.

RAINA (wonderingly). Do you know, you are the first man I ever met who did not take me seriously?

BLUNTSCHLI. You mean, don't you, that I am the first man that has ever taken you quite seriously?

RAINA. Yes, I suppose I do mean that. (Cosily, quite at her ease with him.) How strange it is to be talked to in such a way! You know, I've always gone on like that—I mean the noble attitude and the thrilling voice. I did it when I was a tiny child to my nurse. She believed in it. I do it before my parents. They believe in it. I do it before Sergius. He believes in it.

BLUNTSCHLI. Yes: he's a little in that line himself, isn't he?

RAINA (startled). Do you think so?

BLUNTSCHLI. You know him better than I do.

RAINA. I wonder—I wonder is he? If I thought that—! (Discouraged.) Ah, well, what does it matter? I suppose, now that you've found me out, you despise me.

BLUNTSCHLI (warmly, rising). No, my dear young lady, no, no, no a thousand times. It's part of your youth—part of your charm. I'm like all the rest of them—the nurse—your parents—Sergius: I'm your infatuated admirer.

RAINA (pleased). Really?

BLUNTSCHLI (slapping his breast smartly with his hand, German fashion). Hand aufs Herz! Really and truly.

RAINA (very happy). But what did you think of me for giving you my portrait?

BLUNTSCHLI (astonished). Your portrait! You never gave me your portrait.

RAINA (quickly). Do you mean to say you never got it?

BLUNTSCHLI. No. (He sits down beside her, with renewed interest, and says, with some complacency.) When did you send it to me?

RAINA (indignantly). I did not send it to you. (She turns her head away, and adds, reluctantly.) It was in the pocket of that coat.

BLUNTSCHLI (pursing his lips and rounding his eyes). Oh-o-oh! I never found it. It must be there still.

RAINA (springing up). There still!—for my father to find the first time he puts his hand in his pocket! Oh, how could you be so stupid?

BLUNTSCHLI (rising also). It doesn't matter: it's only a photograph: how can he tell who it was intended for? Tell him he put it there himself.

RAINA (impatiently). Yes, that is so clever—so clever! What shall I do?

BLUNTSCHLI. Ah, I see. You wrote something on it. That was rash!

RAINA (annoyed almost to tears). Oh, to have done such a thing for you, who care no more—except to laugh at me—oh! Are you sure nobody has touched it?

BLUNTSCHLI. Well, I can't be quite sure. You see I couldn't carry it about with me all the time: one can't take much luggage on active service.

RAINA. What did you do with it?

BLUNTSCHLI. When I got through to Peerot I had to put it in safe keeping somehow. I thought of the railway cloak room; but that's the surest place to get looted in modern warfare. So I pawned it.

RAINA. Pawned it!!!

BLUNTSCHLI. I know it doesn't sound nice; but it was much the safest plan. I redeemed it the day before yesterday. Heaven only knows whether the pawnbroker cleared out the pockets or not.

RAINA (furious—throwing the words right into his face). You have a low, shopkeeping mind. You think of things that would never come into a gentleman's head.

BLUNTSCHLI (phlegmatically). That's the Swiss national character, dear lady.

RAINA. Oh, I wish I had never met you. (She flounces away and sits at the window fuming.)

(Louka comes in with a heap of letters and telegrams on her salver, and crosses, with her bold, free gait, to the table. Her left sleeve is looped up to the shoulder with a brooch, shewing her naked arm, with a broad gilt bracelet covering the bruise.)

LOUKA (to Bluntschli). For you. (She empties the salver recklessly on the table.) The messenger is waiting. (She is determined not to be civil to a Servian, even if she must bring him his letters.)

BLUNTSCHLI (to Raina). Will you excuse me: the last postal delivery that reached me was three weeks ago. These are the subsequent accumulations. Four telegrams—a week old. (He opens one.) Oho! Bad news!

RAINA (rising and advancing a little remorsefully). Bad news?

BLUNTSCHLI. My father's dead. (He looks at the telegram with his lips pursed, musing on the unexpected change in his arrangements.)

RAINA. Oh, how very sad!

BLUNTSCHLI. Yes: I shall have to start for home in an hour. He has left a lot of big hotels behind him to be looked after. (Takes up a heavy letter in a long blue envelope.) Here's a whacking letter from the family solicitor. (He pulls out the enclosures and glances over them.) Great Heavens! Seventy! Two hundred! (In a crescendo of dismay.) Four hundred! Four thousand!! Nine thousand six hundred!!! What on earth shall I do with them all?

RAINA (timidly). Nine thousand hotels?

BLUNTSCHLI. Hotels! Nonsense. If you only knew!—oh, it's too ridiculous! Excuse me: I must give my fellow orders about starting. (He leaves the room hastily, with the documents in his hand.)

LOUKA (tauntingly). He has not much heart, that Swiss, though he is so fond of the Servians. He has not a word of grief for his poor father.

RAINA (bitterly). Grief!—a man who has been doing nothing but killing people for years! What does he care? What does any soldier care? (She goes to the door, evidently restraining her tears with difficulty.)

LOUKA. Major Saranoff has been fighting, too; and he has plenty of heart left. (Raina, at the door, looks haughtily at her and goes out.) Aha! I thought you wouldn't get much feeling out of your soldier. (She is following Raina when Nicola enters with an armful of logs for the fire.)

NICOLA (grinning amorously at her). I've been trying all the afternoon to get a minute alone with you, my girl. (His countenance changes as he notices her arm.) Why, what fashion is that of wearing your sleeve, child?

LOUKA (proudly). My own fashion.

NICOLA. Indeed! If the mistress catches you, she'll talk to you. (He throws the logs down on the ottoman, and sits comfortably beside them.)

LOUKA. Is that any reason why you should take it on yourself to talk to me?

NICOLA. Come: don't be so contrary with me. I've some good news for you. (He takes out some paper money. Louka, with an eager gleam in her eyes, comes close to look at it.) See, a twenty leva bill! Sergius gave me that out of pure swagger. A fool and his money are soon parted. There's ten levas more. The Swiss gave me that for backing up the mistress's and Raina's lies about him. He's no fool, he isn't. You should have heard old Catherine downstairs as polite as you please to me, telling me not to mind the Major being a little impatient; for they knew what a good servant I was—after making a fool and a liar of me before them all! The twenty will go to our savings; and you shall have the ten to spend if you'll only talk to me so as to remind me I'm a human being. I get tired of being a servant occasionally.

LOUKA (scornfully). Yes: sell your manhood for thirty levas, and buy me for ten! Keep your money. You were born to be a servant. I was not. When you set up your shop you will only be everybody's servant instead of somebody's servant.

NICOLA (picking up his logs, and going to the stove). Ah, wait till you see. We shall have our evenings to ourselves; and I shall be master in my own house, I promise you. (He throws the logs down and kneels at the stove.)

LOUKA. You shall never be master in mine. (She sits down on Sergius's chair.)

NICOLA (turning, still on his knees, and squatting down rather forlornly, on his calves, daunted by her implacable disdain). You have a great ambition in you, Louka. Remember: if any luck comes to you, it was I that made a woman of you.

LOUKA. You!

NICOLA (with dogged self-assertion). Yes, me. Who was it made you give up wearing a couple of pounds of false black hair on your head and reddening your lips and cheeks like any other Bulgarian girl? I did. Who taught you to trim your nails, and keep your hands clean, and be dainty about yourself, like a fine Russian lady? Me! do you hear that? me! (She tosses her head defiantly; and he rises, ill-humoredly, adding more coolly) I've often thought that if Raina were out of the way, and you just a little less of a fool and Sergius just a little more of one, you might come to be one of my grandest customers, instead of only being my wife and costing me money.

LOUKA. I believe you would rather be my servant than my husband. You would make more out of me. Oh, I know that soul of yours.

NICOLA (going up close to her for greater emphasis). Never you mind my soul; but just listen to my advice. If you want to be a lady, your present behaviour to me won't do at all, unless when we're alone. It's too sharp and imprudent; and impudence is a sort of familiarity: it shews affection for me. And don't you try being high and mighty with me either. You're like all country girls: you think it's genteel to treat a servant the way I treat a stable-boy. That's only your ignorance; and don't you forget it. And don't be so ready to defy everybody. Act as if you expected to have your own way, not as if you expected to be ordered about. The way to get on as a lady is the same as the way to get on as a servant: you've got to know your place; that's the secret of it. And you may depend on me to know my place if you get promoted. Think over it, my girl. I'll stand by you: one servant should always stand by another.

LOUKA (rising impatiently). Oh, I must behave in my own way. You take all the courage out of me with your cold-blooded wisdom. Go and put those logs on the fire: that's the sort of thing you understand. (Before Nicola can retort, Sergius comes in. He checks himself a moment on seeing Louka; then goes to the stove.)

SERGIUS (to Nicola). I am not in the way of your work, I hope.

NICOLA (in a smooth, elderly manner). Oh, no, sir, thank you kindly. I was only speaking to this foolish girl about her habit of running up here to the library whenever she gets a chance, to look at the books. That's the worst of her education, sir: it gives her habits above her station. (To Louka.) Make that table tidy, Louka, for the Major. (He goes out sedately.)

(Louka, without looking at Sergius, begins to arrange the papers on the table. He crosses slowly to her, and studies the arrangement of her sleeve reflectively.)

SERGIUS. Let me see: is there a mark there? (He turns up the bracelet and sees the bruise made by his grasp. She stands motionless, not looking at him: fascinated, but on her guard.) Ffff! Does it hurt?

LOUKA. Yes.

SERGIUS. Shall I cure it?

LOUKA (instantly withdrawing herself proudly, but still not looking at him). No. You cannot cure it now.

SERGIUS (masterfully). Quite sure? (He makes a movement as if to take her in his arms.)

LOUKA. Don't trifle with me, please. An officer should not trifle with a servant.

SERGIUS (touching the arm with a merciless stroke of his forefinger). That was no trifle, Louka.

LOUKA. No. (Looking at him for the first time.) Are you sorry?

SERGIUS (with measured emphasis, folding his arms). I am never sorry.

LOUKA (wistfully). I wish I could believe a man could be so unlike a woman as that. I wonder are you really a brave man?

SERGIUS (unaffectedly, relaxing his attitude). Yes: I am a brave man. My heart jumped like a woman's at the first shot; but in the charge I found that I was brave. Yes: that at least is real about me.

LOUKA. Did you find in the charge that the men whose fathers are poor like mine were any less brave than the men who are rich like you?

SERGIUS (with bitter levity.) Not a bit. They all slashed and cursed and yelled like heroes. Psha! the courage to rage and kill is cheap. I have an English bull terrier who has as much of that sort of courage as the whole Bulgarian nation, and the whole Russian nation at its back. But he lets my groom thrash him, all the same. That's your soldier all over! No, Louka, your poor men can cut throats; but they are afraid of their officers; they put up with insults and blows; they stand by and see one another punished like children—-aye, and help to do it when they are ordered. And the officers!—-well (with a short, bitter laugh) I am an officer. Oh, (fervently) give me the man who will defy to the death any power on earth or in heaven that sets itself up against his own will and conscience: he alone is the brave man.

LOUKA. How easy it is to talk! Men never seem to me to grow up: they all have schoolboy's ideas. You don't know what true courage is.

SERGIUS (ironically). Indeed! I am willing to be instructed.

LOUKA. Look at me! how much am I allowed to have my own will? I have to get your room ready for you—to sweep and dust, to fetch and carry. How could that degrade me if it did not degrade you to have it done for you? But (with subdued passion) if I were Empress of Russia, above everyone in the world, then—ah, then, though according to you I could shew no courage at all; you should see, you should see.

SERGIUS. What would you do, most noble Empress?

LOUKA. I would marry the man I loved, which no other queen in Europe has the courage to do. If I loved you, though you would be as far beneath me as I am beneath you, I would dare to be the equal of my inferior. Would you dare as much if you loved me? No: if you felt the

45

beginnings of love for me you would not let it grow. You dare not: you would marry a rich man's daughter because you would be afraid of what other people would say of you.

SERGIUS (carried away). You lie: it is not so, by all the stars! If I loved you, and I were the Czar himself, I would set you on the throne by my side. You know that I love another woman, a woman as high above you as heaven is above earth. And you are jealous of her.

LOUKA. I have no reason to be. She will never marry you now. The man I told you of has come back. She will marry the Swiss.

SERGIUS (recoiling). The Swiss!

LOUKA. A man worth ten of you. Then you can come to me; and I will refuse you. You are not good enough for me. (She turns to the door.)

SERGIUS (springing after her and catching her fiercely in his arms). I will kill the Swiss; and afterwards I will do as I please with you.

LOUKA (in his arms, passive and steadfast). The Swiss will kill you, perhaps. He has beaten you in love. He may beat you in war.

SERGIUS (tormentedly). Do you think I believe that she—she! whose worst thoughts are higher than your best ones, is capable of trifling with another man behind my back?

LOUKA. Do you think she would believe the Swiss if he told her now that I am in your arms?

SERGIUS (releasing her in despair). Damnation! Oh, damnation! Mockery, mockery everywhere: everything I think is mocked by everything I do. (He strikes himself frantically on the breast.) Coward, liar, fool! Shall I kill myself like a man, or live and pretend to laugh at myself? (She again turns to go.) Louka! (She stops near the door.) Remember: you belong to me.

LOUKA (quietly). What does that mean—an insult?

SERGIUS (commandingly). It means that you love me, and that I have had you here in my arms, and will perhaps have you there again. Whether that is an insult I neither know nor care: take it as you please. But (vehemently) I will not be a coward and a trifler. If I choose to love you, I dare marry you, in spite of all Bulgaria. If these hands ever touch you again, they shall touch my affianced bride.

LOUKA. We shall see whether you dare keep your word. But take care. I will not wait long.

SERGIUS (again folding his arms and standing motionless in the middle of the room). Yes, we shall see. And you shall wait my pleasure.

(Bluntschli, much preoccupied, with his papers still in his hand, enters, leaving the door open for Louka to go out. He goes across to the table, glancing at her as he passes. Sergius, without altering his resolute attitude, watches him steadily. Louka goes out, leaving the door open.)

BLUNTSCHLI (absently, sitting at the table as before, and putting down his papers). That's a remarkable looking young woman.

SERGIUS (gravely, without moving). Captain Bluntschli.

BLUNTSCHLI. Eh?

SERGIUS. You have deceived me. You are my rival. I brook no rivals. At six o'clock I shall be in the drilling-ground on the Klissoura road, alone, on horseback, with my sabre. Do you understand?

BLUNTSCHLI (staring, but sitting quite at his ease). Oh, thank you: that's a cavalry man's proposal. I'm in the artillery; and I have the choice of weapons. If I go, I shall take a machine gun. And there shall be no mistake about the cartridges this time.

SERGIUS (flushing, but with deadly coldness). Take care, sir. It is not our custom in Bulgaria to allow invitations of that kind to be trifled with.

BLUNTSCHLI (warmly). Pooh! don't talk to me about Bulgaria. You don't know what fighting is. But have it your own way. Bring your sabre along. I'll meet you.

SERGIUS (fiercely delighted to find his opponent a man of spirit). Well said, Switzer. Shall I lend you my best horse?

BLUNTSCHLI. No: damn your horse!—-thank you all the same, my dear fellow. (Raina comes in, and hears the next sentence.) I shall fight you on foot. Horseback's too dangerous: I don't want to kill you if I can help it.

RAINA (hurrying forward anxiously). I have heard what Captain Bluntschli said, Sergius. You are going to fight. Why? (Sergius turns away in silence, and goes to the stove, where he stands watching her as she continues, to Bluntschli) What about?

BLUNTSCHLI. I don't know: he hasn't told me. Better not interfere, dear young lady. No harm will be done: I've often acted as sword instructor. He won't be able to touch me; and I'll not hurt him. It will save explanations. In the morning I shall be off home; and you'll never see me or hear of me again. You and he will then make it up and live happily ever after.

RAINA (turning away deeply hurt, almost with a sob in her voice). I never said I wanted to see you again.

SERGIUS (striding forward). Ha! That is a confession.

RAINA (haughtily). What do you mean?

SERGIUS. You love that man!

RAINA (scandalized). Sergius!

SERGIUS. You allow him to make love to you behind my back, just as you accept me as your affianced husband behind his. Bluntschli: you knew our relations; and you deceived me. It is for that that I call you to account, not for having received favours that I never enjoyed.

BLUNTSCHLI (jumping up indignantly). Stuff! Rubbish! I have received no favours. Why, the young lady doesn't even know whether I'm married or not.

RAINA (forgetting herself). Oh! (Collapsing on the ottoman.) Are you?

SERGIUS. You see the young lady's concern, Captain Bluntschli. Denial is useless. You have enjoyed the privilege of being received in her own room, late at night—

BLUNTSCHLI (interrupting him pepperily). Yes; you blockhead! She received me with a pistol at her head. Your cavalry were at my heels. I'd have blown out her brains if she'd uttered a cry.

SERGIUS (taken aback). Bluntschli! Raina: is this true?

RAINA (rising in wrathful majesty). Oh, how dare you, how dare you?

BLUNTSCHLI. Apologize, man, apologize! (He resumes his seat at the table.)

SERGIUS (with the old measured emphasis, folding his arms). I never apologize.

RAINA (passionately). This is the doing of that friend of yours, Captain Bluntschli. It is he who is spreading this horrible story about me. (She walks about excitedly.)

BLUNTSCHLI. No: he's dead—burnt alive.

RAINA (stopping, shocked). Burnt alive!

BLUNTSCHLI. Shot in the hip in a wood yard. Couldn't drag himself out. Your fellows' shells set the timber on fire and burnt him, with half a dozen other poor devils in the same predicament.

RAINA. How horrible!

SERGIUS. And how ridiculous! Oh, war! war! the dream of patriots and heroes! A fraud, Bluntschli, a hollow sham, like love.

RAINA (outraged). Like love! You say that before me.

BLUNTSCHLI. Come, Saranoff: that matter is explained.

SERGIUS. A hollow sham, I say. Would you have come back here if nothing had passed between you, except at the muzzle of your pistol? Raina is mistaken about our friend who was burnt. He was not my informant.

RAINA. Who then? (Suddenly guessing the truth.) Ah, Louka! my maid, my servant! You were with her this morning all that time after—-after—-Oh, what sort of god is this I have been worshipping! (He meets her gaze with sardonic enjoyment of her disenchantment. Angered all the more, she goes closer to him, and says, in a lower, intenser tone) Do you know that I looked out of the window as I went upstairs, to have another sight of my hero; and I saw something that I did not understand then. I know now that you were making love to her.

SERGIUS (with grim humor). You saw that?

RAINA. Only too well. (She turns away, and throws herself on the divan under the centre window, quite overcome.)

SERGIUS (cynically). Raina: our romance is shattered. Life's a farce.

BLUNTSCHLI (to Raina, goodhumoredly). You see: he's found himself out now.

SERGIUS. Bluntschli: I have allowed you to call me a blockhead. You may now call me a coward as well. I refuse to fight you. Do you know why?

BLUNTSCHLI. No; but it doesn't matter. I didn't ask the reason when you cried on; and I don't ask the reason now that you cry off. I'm a professional soldier. I fight when I have to, and am very glad to get out of it when I haven't to. You're only an amateur: you think fighting's an amusement.

SERGIUS. You shall hear the reason all the same, my professional. The reason is that it takes two men—real men—men of heart, blood and honor—to make a genuine combat. I could no more fight with you than I could make love to an ugly woman. You've no magnetism: you're not a man, you're a machine.

BLUNTSCHLI (apologetically). Quite true, quite true. I always was that sort of chap. I'm very sorry. But now that you've found that life isn't a farce, but something quite sensible and serious, what further obstacle is there to your happiness?

RAINA (riling). You are very solicitous about my happiness and his. Do you forget his new love—Louka? It is not you that he must fight now, but his rival, Nicola.

SERGIUS. Rival!! (Striking his forehead.)

RAINA. Did you not know that they are engaged?

SERGIUS. Nicola! Are fresh abysses opening! Nicola!!

RAINA (sarcastically). A shocking sacrifice, isn't it? Such beauty, such intellect, such modesty, wasted on a middle-aged servant man! Really, Sergius, you cannot stand by and allow such a thing. It would be unworthy of your chivalry.

SERGIUS (losing all self-control). Viper! Viper! (He rushes to and fro, raging.)

BLUNTSCHLI. Look here, Saranoff; you're getting the worst of this.

RAINA (getting angrier). Do you realize what he has done, Captain Bluntschli? He has set this girl as a spy on us; and her reward is that he makes love to her.

SERGIUS. False! Monstrous!

RAINA. Monstrous! (Confronting him.) Do you deny that she told you about Captain Bluntschli being in my room?

SERGIUS. No; but—

RAINA (interrupting). Do you deny that you were making love to her when she told you?

SERGIUS. No; but I tell you—

RAINA (cutting him short contemptuously). It is unnecessary to tell us anything more. That is quite enough for us. (She turns her back on him and sweeps majestically back to the window.)

BLUNTSCHLI (quietly, as Sergius, in an agony of mortification, rinks on the ottoman, clutching his averted head between his fists). I told you you were getting the worst of it, Saranoff.

SERGIUS. Tiger cat!

RAINA (running excitedly to Bluntschli). You hear this man calling me names, Captain Bluntschli?

BLUNTSCHLI. What else can he do, dear lady? He must defend himself somehow. Come (very persuasively), don't quarrel. What good does it do? (Raina, with a gasp, sits down on the ottoman, and after a vain effort to look vexedly at Bluntschli, she falls a victim to her sense of humor, and is attacked with a disposition to laugh.)

SERGIUS. Engaged to Nicola! (He rises.) Ha! ha! (Going to the stove and standing with his back to it.) Ah, well, Bluntschli, you are right to take this huge imposture of a world coolly.

RAINA (to Bluntschli with an intuitive guess at his state of mind). I daresay you think us a couple of grown up babies, don't you?

SERGIUS (grinning a little). He does, he does. Swiss civilization nursetending Bulgarian barbarism, eh?

BLUNTSCHLI (blushing). Not at all, I assure you. I'm only very glad to get you two quieted. There now, let's be pleasant and talk it over in a friendly way. Where is this other young lady?

RAINA. Listening at the door, probably.

SERGIUS (shivering as if a bullet had struck him, and speaking with quiet but deep indignation). I will prove that that, at least, is a calumny. (He goes with dignity to the door and opens it. A yell of fury bursts from him as he looks out. He darts into the passage, and returns dragging in Louka, whom he flings against the table, R., as he cries) Judge her, Bluntschli—you, the moderate, cautious man: judge the eavesdropper.

(Louka stands her ground, proud and silent.)

BLUNTSCHLI (shaking his head). I mustn't judge her. I once listened myself outside a tent when there was a mutiny brewing. It's all a question of the degree of provocation. My life was at stake.

LOUKA. My love was at stake. (Sergius flinches, ashamed of her in spite of himself.) I am not ashamed.

RAINA (contemptuously). Your love! Your curiosity, you mean.

LOUKA (facing her and retorting her contempt with interest). My love, stronger than anything you can feel, even for your chocolate cream soldier.

SERGIUS (with quick suspicion—to Louka). What does that mean?

LOUKA (fiercely). It means—

SERGIUS (interrupting her slightingly). Oh, I remember, the ice pudding. A paltry taunt, girl.

(Major Petkoff enters, in his shirtsleeves.)

PETKOFF. Excuse my shirtsleeves, gentlemen. Raina: somebody has been wearing that coat of mine: I'll swear it—somebody with bigger shoulders than mine. It's all burst open at the back. Your mother is mending it. I wish she'd make haste. I shall catch cold. (He looks more attentively at them.) Is anything the matter?

RAINA. No. (She sits down at the stove with a tranquil air.)

SERGIUS. Oh, no! (He sits down at the end of the table, as at first.)

BLUNTSCHLI (who is already seated). Nothing, nothing.

PETKOFF (sitting down on the ottoman in his old place). That's all right. (He notices Louka.) Anything the matter, Louka?

LOUKA. No, sir.

PETKOFF (genially). That's all right. (He sneezes.) Go and ask your mistress for my coat, like a good girl, will you? (She turns to obey; but Nicola enters with the coat; and she makes a pretence of having business in the room by taking the little table with the hookah away to the wall near the windows.)

RAINA (rising quickly, as she sees the coat on Nicola's arm). Here it is, papa. Give it to me, Nicola; and do you put some more wood on the fire. (She takes the coat, and brings it to the Major, who stands up to put it on. Nicola attends to the fire.)

PETKOFF (to Raina, teasing her affectionately). Aha! Going to be very good to poor old papa just for one day after his return from the wars, eh?

RAINA (with solemn reproach). Ah, how can you say that to me, father?

PETKOFF. Well, well, only a joke, little one. Come, give me a kiss. (She kisses him.) Now give me the coat.

RAINA. Now, I am going to put it on for you. Turn your back. (He turns his back and feels behind him with his arms for the sleeves. She dexterously takes the photograph from the pocket and throws it on the table before Bluntschli, who covers it with a sheet of paper under the very nose of Sergius, who looks on amazed, with his suspicions roused in the highest degree. She then helps Petkoff on with his coat.) There, dear! Now are you comfortable?

PETKOFF. Quite, little love. Thanks. (He sits down; and Raina returns to her seat near the stove.) Oh, by the bye, I've found something funny. What's the meaning of this? (He put his hand into the picked pocket.) Eh? Hallo! (He tries the other pocket.) Well, I could have sworn—(Much puzzled, he tries the breast pocket.) I wonder—(Tries the original pocket.) Where can it—(A light flashes on him; he rises, exclaiming) Your mother's taken it.

RAINA (very red). Taken what?

PETKOFF. Your photograph, with the inscription: "Raina, to her Chocolate Cream Soldier—a souvenir." Now you know there's something more in this than meets the eye; and I'm going to find it out. (Shouting) Nicola!

NICOLA (dropping a log, and turning). Sir!

PETKOFF. Did you spoil any pastry of Miss Raina's this morning?

NICOLA. You heard Miss Raina say that I did, sir.

PETKOFF. I know that, you idiot. Was it true?

NICOLA. I am sure Miss Raina is incapable of saying anything that is not true, sir.

PETKOFF. Are you? Then I'm not. (Turning to the others.) Come: do you think I don't see it all? (Goes to Sergius, and slaps him on the shoulder.) Sergius: you're the chocolate cream soldier, aren't you?

SERGIUS (starting up). I! a chocolate cream soldier! Certainly not.

PETKOFF. Not! (He looks at them. They are all very serious and very conscious.) Do you mean to tell me that Raina sends photographic souvenirs to other men?

SERGIUS (enigmatically). The world is not such an innocent place as we used to think, Petkoff.

BLUNTSCHLI (rising). It's all right, Major. I'm the chocolate cream soldier. (Petkoff and Sergius are equally astonished.) The gracious young lady saved my life by giving me chocolate creams when I was starving—shall I ever forget their flavour! My late friend Stolz told you the story at Peerot. I was the fugitive.

PETKOFF. You! (He gasps.) Sergius: do you remember how those two women went on this morning when we mentioned it? (Sergius smiles cynically. Petkoff confronts Raina severely.) You're a nice young woman, aren't you?

RAINA (bitterly). Major Saranoff has changed his mind. And when I wrote that on the photograph, I did not know that Captain Bluntschli was married.

BLUNTSCHLI (much startled protesting vehemently). I'm not married.

RAINA (with deep reproach). You said you were.

BLUNTSCHLI. I did not. I positively did not. I never was married in my life.

PETKOFF (exasperated). Raina: will you kindly inform me, if I am not asking too much, which gentleman you are engaged to?

RAINA. To neither of them. This young lady (introducing Louka, who faces them all proudly) is the object of Major Saranoff's affections at present.

PETKOFF. Louka! Are you mad, Sergius? Why, this girl's engaged to Nicola.

NICOLA (coming forward). I beg your pardon, sir. There is a mistake. Louka is not engaged to me.

PETKOFF. Not engaged to you, you scoundrel! Why, you had twenty-five levas from me on the day of your betrothal; and she had that gilt bracelet from Miss Raina.

NICOLA (with cool unction). We gave it out so, sir. But it was only to give Louka protection. She had a soul above her station; and I have been no more than her confidential servant. I intend, as you know, sir, to set up a shop later on in Sofia; and I look forward to her custom and recommendation should she marry into the nobility. (He goes out with impressive discretion, leaving them all staring after him.)

PETKOFF (breaking the silence). Well, I am—-hm!

SERGIUS. This is either the finest heroism or the most crawling baseness. Which is it, Bluntschli?

BLUNTSCHLI. Never mind whether it's heroism or baseness. Nicola's the ablest man I've met in Bulgaria. I'll make him manager of a hotel if he can speak French and German.

LOUKA (suddenly breaking out at Sergius). I have been insulted by everyone here. You set them the example. You owe me an apology. (Sergius immediately, like a repeating clock of which the spring has been touched, begins to fold his arms.)

BLUNTSCHLI (before he can speak). It's no use. He never apologizes.

LOUKA. Not to you, his equal and his enemy. To me, his poor servant, he will not refuse to apologize.

SERGIUS (approvingly). You are right. (He bends his knee in his grandest manner.) Forgive me!

LOUKA. I forgive you. (She timidly gives him her hand, which he kisses.) That touch makes me your affianced wife.

SERGIUS (springing up). Ah, I forgot that!

LOUKA (coldly). You can withdraw if you like.

SERGIUS. Withdraw! Never! You belong to me! (He puts his arm about her and draws her to him.) (Catherine comes in and finds Louka in Sergius's arms, and all the rest gazing at them in bewildered astonishment.)

CATHERINE. What does this mean? (Sergius releases Louka.)

PETKOFF. Well, my dear, it appears that Sergius is going to marry Louka instead of Raina. (She is about to break out indignantly at him: he stops her by exclaiming testily.) Don't blame me: I've nothing to do with it. (He retreats to the stove.)

CATHERINE. Marry Louka! Sergius: you are bound by your word to us!

SERGIUS (folding his arms). Nothing binds me.

BLUNTSCHLI (much pleased by this piece of common sense). Saranoff: your hand. My congratulations. These heroics of yours have their practical side after all. (To Louka.) Gracious young lady: the best wishes of a good Republican! (He kisses her hand, to Raina's great disgust.)

CATHERINE (threateningly). Louka: you have been telling stories.

LOUKA. I have done Raina no harm.

CATHERINE (haughtily). Raina! (Raina is equally indignant at the liberty.)

LOUKA. I have a right to call her Raina: she calls me Louka. I told Major Saranoff she would never marry him if the Swiss gentleman came back.

BLUNTSCHLI (surprised). Hallo!

LOUKA (turning to Raina). I thought you were fonder of him than of Sergius. You know best whether I was right.

BLUNTSCHLI. What nonsense! I assure you, my dear Major, my dear Madame, the gracious young lady simply saved my life, nothing else. She never cared two straws for me. Why, bless my heart and soul, look at the young lady and look at me. She, rich, young, beautiful, with her imagination full of fairy princes and noble natures and cavalry charges and goodness knows what! And I, a common-place Swiss soldier who hardly knows what a decent life is after fifteen years of barracks and battles—a vagabond—a man who has spoiled all his chances in life through an incurably romantic disposition—a man—

SERGIUS (starting as if a needle had pricked him and interrupting Bluntschli in incredulous amazement). Excuse me, Bluntschli: what did you say had spoiled your chances in life?

BLUNTSCHLI (promptly). An incurably romantic disposition. I ran away from home twice when I was a boy. I went into the army instead of into my father's business. I climbed the balcony of this house when a man of sense would have dived into the nearest cellar. I came sneaking back here to have another look at the young lady when any other man of my age would have sent the coat back—

PETKOFF. My coat!

BLUNTSCHLI.—Yes: that's the coat I mean—would have sent it back and gone quietly home. Do you suppose I am the sort of fellow a young girl falls in love with? Why, look at our ages! I'm thirty-four: I don't suppose the young lady is much over seventeen. (This estimate produces a marked sensation, all the rest turning and staring at one another. He proceeds innocently.) All that adventure which was life or death to me, was only a schoolgirl's game to her—chocolate creams and hide and seek. Here's the proof! (He takes the photograph from the table.) Now, I ask you, would a woman who took the affair seriously have sent me this and written on it: "Raina, to her chocolate cream soldier—a souvenir"? (He exhibits the photograph triumphantly, as if it settled the matter beyond all possibility of refutation.)

PETKOFF. That's what I was looking for. How the deuce did it get there?

BLUNTSCHLI (to Raina complacently). I have put everything right, I hope, gracious young lady!

RAINA (in uncontrollable vexation). I quite agree with your account of yourself. You are a romantic idiot. (Bluntschli is unspeakably taken aback.) Next time I hope you will know the difference between a schoolgirl of seventeen and a woman of twenty-three.

BLUNTSCHLI (stupefied). Twenty-three! (She snaps the photograph contemptuously from his hand; tears it across; and throws the pieces at his feet.)

SERGIUS (with grim enjoyment of Bluntschli's discomfiture). Bluntschli: my one last belief is gone. Your sagacity is a fraud, like all the other things. You have less sense than even I have.

BLUNTSCHLI (overwhelmed). Twenty-three! Twenty-three!! (He considers.) Hm! (Swiftly making up his mind.) In that case, Major Petkoff, I beg to propose formally to become a suitor for your daughter's hand, in place of Major Saranoff retired.

RAINA. You dare!

BLUNTSCHLI. If you were twenty-three when you said those things to me this afternoon, I shall take them seriously.

CATHERINE (loftily polite). I doubt, sir, whether you quite realize either my daughter's position or that of Major Sergius Saranoff, whose place you propose to take. The Petkoffs and the Saranoffs are known as the richest and most important families in the country. Our position is almost historical: we can go back for nearly twenty years.

PETKOFF. Oh, never mind that, Catherine. (To Bluntschli.) We should be most happy, Bluntschli, if it were only a question of your position; but hang it, you know, Raina is accustomed to a very comfortable establishment. Sergius keeps twenty horses.

BLUNTSCHLI. But what on earth is the use of twenty horses? Why, it's a circus.

CATHERINE (severely). My daughter, sir, is accustomed to a first-rate stable.

RAINA. Hush, mother, you're making me ridiculous.

BLUNTSCHLI. Oh, well, if it comes to a question of an establishment, here goes! (He goes impetuously to the table and seizes the papers in the blue envelope.) How many horses did you say?

SERGIUS. Twenty, noble Switzer!

BLUNTSCHLI. I have two hundred horses. (They are amazed.) How many carriages?

SERGIUS. Three.

BLUNTSCHLI. I have seventy. Twenty-four of them will hold twelve inside, besides two on the box, without counting the driver and conductor. How many tablecloths have you?

SERGIUS. How the deuce do I know?

BLUNTSCHLI. Have you four thousand?

SERGIUS. NO.

BLUNTSCHLI. I have. I have nine thousand six hundred pairs of sheets and blankets, with two thousand four hundred eider-down quilts. I have ten thousand knives and forks, and the same quantity of dessert spoons. I have six hundred servants. I have six palatial establishments, besides two livery stables, a tea garden and a private house. I have four medals for distinguished services; I have the rank of an officer and the standing of a gentleman; and I have three native languages. Show me any man in Bulgaria that can offer as much.

PETKOFF (with childish awe). Are you Emperor of Switzerland?

BLUNTSCHLI. My rank is the highest known in Switzerland: I'm a free citizen.

CATHERINE. Then Captain Bluntschli, since you are my daughter's choice, I shall not stand in the way of her happiness. (Petkoff is about to speak.) That is Major Petkoff's feeling also.

PETKOFF. Oh, I shall be only too glad. Two hundred horses! Whew!

SERGIUS. What says the lady?

RAINA (pretending to sulk). The lady says that he can keep his tablecloths and his omnibuses. I am not here to be sold to the highest bidder.

BLUNTSCHLI. I won't take that answer. I appealed to you as a fugitive, a beggar, and a starving man. You accepted me. You gave me your hand to kiss, your bed to sleep in, and your roof to shelter me—

RAINA (interrupting him). I did not give them to the Emperor of Switzerland!

BLUNTSCHLI. That's just what I say. (He catches her hand quickly and looks her straight in the face as he adds, with confident mastery) Now tell us who you did give them to.

RAINA (succumbing with a shy smile). To my chocolate cream soldier!

BLUNTSCHLI (with a boyish laugh of delight). That'll do. Thank you. (Looks at his watch and suddenly becomes businesslike.) Time's up, Major. You've managed those regiments so well that you are sure to be asked to get rid of some of the Infantry of the Teemok division. Send them home by way of Lom Palanka. Saranoff: don't get married until I come back: I shall be here punctually at five in the evening on Tuesday fortnight. Gracious ladies—good evening. (He makes them a military bow, and goes.)

SERGIUS. What a man! What a man!

15787604R00035

Made in the USA
Lexington, KY
16 June 2012